MURDER IN BELGRAVIA

A GINGER GOLD MYSTERY BOOK 16

LEE STRAUSS

Library and Archives Canada Cataloguing in Publication

Title: Murder in Belgravia / Lee Strauss.

Names: Strauss, Lee (Novelist), author.

Series: Strauss, Lee (Novelist). Ginger Gold mystery ; 16.

Description: Series statement: A Ginger Gold mystery ; 16 | "A 1920s cozy historical mystery."

Identifiers: Canadiana (print) 20200404458 | Canadiana (ebook) 20200404466 | ISBN 9781774091548

(hardcover) | ISBN 9781774091531 (softcover) | ISBN 9781774091555 (IngramSpark softcover) | ISBN

9781774091579 (Kindle) | ISBN 9781774091562 (EPUB)

Classification: LCC PS8637.T739 M877 2021 | DDC C813/.6—dc23

❀ Created with Vellum

Murder in Hyde Park
Murder at the Royal Albert Hall
Murder in Belgravia
Murder on Mallowan Court

There was nothing like a good wedding to get the blood pumping and the nerves rattling, even if you weren't the one getting married.

"I remember your wedding day, Mrs. Reed."

Ginger, known as Lady Gold when working in her capacity as a private investigator, smiled at her maid, Lizzie.

"Two years ago, now," Ginger said with a nod. "It's hard to believe we're racing to the end of 1926."

Lizzie flipped through Ginger's wardrobe in the large bedroom on the upper floor of Hartigan House, Ginger's Kensington home. Removing a lovely yellow-velvet drop-waist dress with a handkerchief hem, embellished with gold embroidery, and a large velour bow on the hip, she held it up for Ginger to see.

"It came in just in time, madam," Lizzie said. A petite girl with short, mousy-brown hair pinned under her maid's cap, Lizzie fussed over the gown they had chosen earlier. "It will do the trick nicely. And the colour goes so well with your red hair."

The "trick", of course, was to conceal Ginger's growing belly, helped by the loose fit and dark colour, the child due in a month. Most ladies never ventured out in public when their condition was so obvious, but she wasn't about to miss the nuptials of her former sister-in-law Felicia and Lord Davenport-Witt—not for the world.

Lizzie tittered on as she helped Ginger into the gown. "Weddings are so exciting. Yours and Mr. Reed's was the last one I went to. So lovely. Even if I almost ruined the whole thing!"

"Shh," Ginger said, even though an unfortunate misunderstanding involving her maid had nearly caused a delay. "All's well that ends well."

Lizzie finished fastening the back of the gown. "You're so kind, madam. I honestly can't believe you didn't sack me then."

"And how happy I am that I had no need."

Lizzie, young and spritely, was one of those rare

finds with maids. Cheerful, grateful, and good with children and dogs.

As if he could read her mind, Boss, Ginger's seven-year-old Boston terrier, raised his chin from his position on her four-poster bed where he'd been curled up on the gold, textured quilt in a long nap.

After donning a long white-pearl necklace and matching earrings, Ginger sashayed across the Persian carpet centred on the wooden floor as if for her dog's benefit. "What do you think, Boss? Will it do?"

She paused in front of the full-length mirror tilted on its frame in the room's corner. Trimmed in elaborately carved wood, the mirror matched the bed frame and chests of drawers. Ginger appraised her reflection; she looked like she'd swallowed a large melon. It was a good thing she carried low. "With a shawl and a large, well-placed handbag, no one shall be the wiser."

Ginger might misguide the wedding guests, but her aching back wasn't fooled. Placing her palms on the aching lower back, she settled into one of the gold and white striped chairs that flanked a small table. By the tall south-facing windows, Ginger turned toward the low-intensity of the morning autumn sun.

The bride-to-be was on her mind. Felicia was the

younger sister of Ginger's late husband, Daniel, Lord Gold. Like an older sister, Ginger had taken Felicia under her wing—there was a decade between them—and, more recently, as a friend.

Felicia would soon be a married lady, and Ginger was happy for her.

She was.

The Earl of Witt, known as Lord Davenport-Witt, and Charles to them now, was a decent man. Felicia's elder by a decade, the earl was moneyed and titled with his reputation intact. Ambrosia, known as the Dowager Lady Gold and Felicia's grandmother, was ecstatic.

None of them knew what Ginger knew about the earl. She and Charles had more in common than anyone knew; the two were keepers of secrets. Each other's, and the Crown's.

"Madam?"

Lizzie's voice brought Ginger's thoughts to the present. "Are you all right, madam? Should I fetch some tea?"

A pot of tea wouldn't put off the inevitable.

"It's quite all right, Lizzie. I think I'll see how the bride is doing."

"Yes, madam. The excitement from down the hall has ended now that her bridesmaids have gone."

Having helped Felicia get ready, her six brides-maids had left taking their giggles and teasing with them. Ginger hadn't been invited for the pre-preparation and felt a twinge of hurt when she'd first discovered that. However, Ginger placed a hand on her belly, smiling at the movement going on there. She could see how she'd become more of a mother figure than a sister, and Felicia had asked her to help with her veil before they left.

Ginger checked her wristwatch. It was time to check up on Felicia.

Basil Reed found refuge playing football with his son, Scout, in the back garden of Hartigan House. When he'd married Ginger, he'd made peace with sharing a home with several strong-minded ladies and their maids. A few more had been recently added, but he'd lost track. But with a wedding in the mix, there was too much feminine energy for the men in the house to bear. Clement, the gardener and sometimes chauffeur, busied himself raking autumn leaves. Pippins, the only other male member of staff, hovered by the door at the furthest boundary possible, keeping himself available to Ginger.

Ginger kept those duties light. In her mind,

Pippins, nearing eighty years old, the butler at Hartigan House when she was a child, was more family than staff. Basil admired the man's mettle. Pippins' cornflower-blue eyes always sparkled, even as he kept his expression neutral.

When they stopped for a rest, Pippins, with a slight bow, asked, "Shall I bring out some lemonade, sir?"

"That would be splendid, Pippins, thank you."

Basil felt a twinge of guilt about adding more work to all the bustle in the kitchen, and he hoped the cook, Mrs. Beasley, would overlook his intrusion.

He needn't have worried, as Pippins quickly returned and placed a tray containing two glasses and a jug, beading from the cold beverage inside it, and placed it on the patio table.

"Do we have to go to the silly wedding, Dad?" Scout said after gulping half his glass. The lad nearly wiped his mouth with his sleeve before Basil stopped him, handing him a napkin from a pile sitting on the tray instead. The boy had lived much of his life on the streets before Basil and Ginger adopted him, but some habits refused to die.

"Yes, we do, and weddings aren't silly. Your aunt is very excited, so we must be on our best behaviour to support her."

Scout pouted as only preadolescent lads could. "Yes, Dad."

Basil settled into one of the patio chairs. Even though the nights were getting chilly, they'd been gifted with a few warm autumn days, and fortunately, this was one of them. It wouldn't last for long. "I suppose we'll have to put the back garden to bed," he said to Pippins.

Pippins agreed. "Clement and I have spoken about it, sir. We decided to wait until after the wedding."

"A good decision, indeed."

Basil inhaled the crisp air and exhaled—perhaps to fortify himself to endure all the festivities to come: the ceremony at St. George's Church and the party afterward at Charles' house in Belgravia. It wasn't the wedding plans that had him feeling nervous— Charles seemed a fine chap, and Felicia was happier than a clam—it was that Ginger, after seeing the guest list, had asked him to provide security. Just a couple of constables, she'd said, just in case.

When he'd asked, in case of what, she'd waved him off and changed the subject. *Quite expertly*, he thought, by bringing his hand to her stomach to feel the outline of the baby's foot.

Later, when he examined the guest list for

himself, he could find nothing that would cause alarm, no names of note or notoriety.

He knew Ginger well. If she asked for something out of the ordinary, such as wanting the police to attend the wedding of familial or friendship connections, where the bride and groom were of the noble class, then she had her reasons. Braxton and Newman had agreed to come in the guise of footmen, Newman for the free meal served below stairs, and Braxton out of curiosity. Braxton had fancied Felicia at one time, though that socially uneven coupling had never had a chance.

Basil glanced at his watch then turned to Scout. "Time to get our suits on. I promised your mum I'd get you ready." He'd negotiated with Ginger when he suggested he and Scout could play outside for a while.

"But—"

"No buts." Basil got to his feet. "Let's go. Chop-chop."

eeling a little uncomfortable in her Italian T-strap shoes—everything seemed swollen and at least a size larger than normal —Ginger headed down the wide corridor to Felicia's room. She felt a wave of sadness, knowing that when Felicia returned from her wedding journey, she'd no longer occupy this bedroom nor live in this house. However, Charles had a house on Wilton Crescent in Belgravia where the couple would live. And thank goodness it was only a hop, skip, and a jump away.

Ambrosia stepped into the corridor from her bedroom at the same time. The Dowager Lady Gold's watery blue eyes, framed with wrinkles and folding skin, focused on Ginger. The dowager's hair —the one thing that came close to moving on from the Victorian era–was short with finger waves showing from beneath a dark-green hat. Wearing a matching green gown printed with large bouquets of roses, she stood straight in a manner only possible with the help of a corset, an archaic device Ginger had been happy to discard for the greater good of the feminist cause. Her former grandmother-in-law leaned on a silver-handled walking stick, her fingers adorned with large baubled rings, should anyone doubt she was a lady of stature.

Ginger and Ambrosia hadn't always seen eye to eye, and at this moment, it seemed they were at odds again. It had been Ambrosia's single-minded goal to see her granddaughter married properly, and now that day had come. Ginger, however, would've selected a less complicated man for Felicia, but alas, the choice wasn't hers to make.

"Are you ready, Grandmother?" Ginger said when they met at Felicia's door. She linked her arm with the family matriarch and knocked. "Felicia? May we come in?"

"Yes, please."

Ginger caught a note of emotion in Felicia's voice and cast a glance at Ambrosia.

"Just pre-marriage jitters, that's all," Ambrosia said.

Ginger pushed the door open and stepped inside before Ambrosia. Sitting on her dressing table stool, Felicia stared into her mirror with red-rimmed eyes. Her playful helpmates were gone.

As if Felicia had caught Ginger's look in the mirror's reflection, she explained, "I've sent them away." She turned and took Ginger's hand. "They're really too flighty for me at this moment. I just want time to reflect. This is the end of a chapter of my life, and you and Grandmama are the ones I want to spend it with."

Ginger squeezed Felicia's hand. "Life is full of chapter endings and beginnings. You'll do well in this next one."

Ambrosia settled in a pink-velour chair, a remnant from Felicia's childhood. "Too much sentiment is unhelpful. Felicia, it's time for you to mature into marriage and a family, and none too soon, if you ask me."

Ambrosia's brashness was a quality that one was either dismayed by or admired. Few got away with saying whatever was on their mind. And since learning the truth about Ambrosia's own heartbreak as a young lady—through a sad affair at the Royal Albert Hall—Ginger had extended as much grace as possible.

"Please stand up," Ginger said, "and let me see your gown." Felicia had wanted to go to Paris to shop for her gown, but Ginger's doctor had cautioned against her traveling at this stage of her pregnancy, so instead she'd ordered it from Paris through her shop contacts at Feathers & Flair. Felicia had been disappointed at first, refusing to go without Ginger, but had been well-pleased when the dress had arrived and she saw it first hand.

Seeing it on Felicia now, made Ginger gasp. "Simply stunning," she said. "Both the bride and the dress."

"It reminds me of Lady Elizabeth Bowes-Lyon's gown when she married Prince Albert, Duke of York," Felicia said. The loosely fitted satin gown had a lace bodice, a low waist, and satin and sheer layers for the skirt which rested on the top of her white shoes.

Felicia returned to her stool and took a deep breath. "I'm ready for my veil, Ginger."

Ginger removed the delicate veil from the box, took the headpiece and placed it on Felicia's auburn, marcelled waves. Fitting snugly, the veil had a gorgeous lace trim that added a softness to Felicia's face. Ginger guided Felicia to her feet and spread the veil across her shoulders, letting the rest of it pool onto the floor.

"Oh, Felicia," Ginger said. "You're exquisite."

The long train prevented a full turn, but Felicia took a couple of steps towards Ambrosia, who nodded in approval.

"Beautiful," she offered.

Felicia beamed. "Thank you, Grandmama."

Ambrosia had stepped in as both grandmother and mother to Felicia and her brother Daniel when their parents had been tragically killed in a carriage accident. The relationship between the two ladies hadn't often been easy, but their love for each other had never been in question.

Felicia regarded her reflection in the full-length mirror, and to Ginger's great surprise, burst into tears.

"Felicia, darling," Ginger said gently. "Are you having a change of heart?"

Though it would be dreadfully embarrassing to call off the wedding, Ginger felt a tingle of relief at the thought.

Ambrosia's round eyes widened in alarm. "Don't be silly. It's perfectly natural for one to have cold feet before a wedding. Once tomorrow arrives, she'll be fine."

Felicia dabbed under her eyes with a handkerchief. "I mustn't ruin my make-up."

"Felicia?" Ginger prodded.

"I'm fine, Ginger. And I don't have cold feet. In fact, I'm perfectly happy. I just can't believe this is finally happening for me. *I'm* getting married. To Charles! And I love him!"

"And he loves you," Ginger replied graciously. "Now, unless you want to keep your groom waiting, we should get ourselves ready to go."

$\mathcal{A}$mbrosia had asked for a minute alone with Felicia, so Ginger headed down the grand curving staircase that opened onto the black-and-white tiles of the entrance hall. Immediately in front of her were the tall, heavy wooden doors that led to the front garden. To her left, French doors opened from the entrance to the drawing room, and on the right side was the sitting room. Above, hanging from the vaulted ceiling, a large electric chandelier cast jewel-like lighting about the room.

Like wind in a mini wind tunnel, Scout entered from the corridor at the back portion of the house and scampered up the stairs.

"Excuse me, Mum," he said.

"Scout! You're not even ready?"

"Going to do that now, Mum," he returned from the top landing.

Ginger snorted then saw Basil coming in after her son. She feigned displeasure. "You said you'd get the two of you ready on time."

Basil made a show of checking his wristwatch. "Ah, yes. Ten minutes until the chariot leaves." He grinned, and the lines around his hazel eyes deepened. "Plenty of time."

"Basil!"

He ran up the stairs, taking them two at a time. "We'll be ready!"

Boss took that moment to skip down the stairs.

"Look at you, the first to be ready to go, and you aren't even invited." Ginger hung on to the banister to balance herself as she crouched to pat her dog. "Lizzie has a treat waiting for you in the kitchen, so you won't even notice."

Pippins, in his mysterious way, appeared as if out of nowhere. "Might I be of assistance, madam?"

Ginger considered her butler with fondness. Of all the members of her household, she'd known and loved him the longest.

"It seems I'm the only one ready to go to this wedding, Pips. Even the bride is lagging. Are the motorcars ready?"

"Yes, madam," Pippins said. "Clement has the Crossley and the Austin parked out the front, ready to go."

"So good of him."

Basil had a splendid motorcar in the forest green Austin 7 he drove, but Ginger's Crossley, with its shiny white exterior and red leather interior, made for a much more glamorous wedding vehicle, so for today, Basil would use it to transport Felicia to the church whilst Ginger, Scout and Ambrosia would be chauffeured by Clement in the Austin.

As promised, Basil and Scout appeared in time, both looking dapper in their matching morning suits, with Basil having the addition of a gold tie pin and a duck-egg blue waistcoat. Scout in black tails and grey trousers gave Ginger a glimpse of her son's future at Eton or Oxford and a smile spread widely across her face. She was thankful that professional photographers had been hired for the celebration. Still, for this sweet moment, her memory would have to snap the image for her to treasure for all eternity.

She clapped her hands together. "You gentlemen look divine!"

By the time they made it to the foot of the staircase, the house staff had gathered to wish Felicia well before she left, stretched in a line according to seniority: Pippins, Mrs. Beasley, Clement, Ambrosia's tall and angular maid Langley, and Lizzie along with the newest maids to join the house. Soon, Ginger realised she'd have to add to their number, as a nurse and nanny would be needed shortly.

The group watched the landing in anticipation and were soon rewarded. Ambrosia appeared first, then Felicia stepped in beside her.

The two Gold ladies leaned on each other as they managed the stairs, the women beaming and lovely. Felicia looked angelic in her layers of lace and silk. The family was stunned by her beauty, and Scout even let out an uncharacteristic, "*Lumme*," his interest in the opposite sex only recently aroused.

Basil stepped forward to take Felicia's arm as Ginger did the same for Ambrosia. Pippins opened the front door.

"Farewell," he said. "I wish you joy!"

The rest of the staff echoed him, "Farewell. We wish you joy!"

Felicia smiled and waved a hand at them all. "Thank you, everyone!"

Ginger sat in the passenger seat of the Austin, with Ambrosia and Scout in the back. Basil, with Felicia looking radiant beside him, started the engine of the Crossley and honked the horn as he followed

Clement in circling the cul-de-sac of Mallowan Court. Ginger turned back to see Felicia stare back at Hartigan House as if she were saying goodbye to the limestone structure with its wrought-iron fence.

Ginger supposed she was. They had already arranged for Charles' servants to move her things while they were away on their wedding journey to Greece.

Ginger turned away, shielding her face with her gloved hand. She could at least wait until the ceremony started before permitting the tears to roll.

St. George's Church in the city of London was not in Ginger's parish of Kensington, but she'd crossed borders to attend ever since she, her fellow-redhead Reverend Oliver Hill, and his wife, Matilda, had become friends. The wedding of an earl and the daughter of a baron was a societal thrill, and a crowd had formed outside the doors, a sea of bowler and cloche hats, and pushed to the main road. Police on horseback tried to control the throng, making way for their motorcars to reach the church's front doors. The eighteenth-century limestone structure had a square, turret-like tower rather than a steeple, rising high over the front doors. Ginger, Scout, and Ambrosia safely made their way inside the nave through the main doors. Basil would sneak the bride in from one of the more obscure side entrances.

Inside, the nave filled with a prism of colour as the late-morning light pierced the stained-glass windows that ran the length of the church on both sides. The windows produced a sense of awe and holiness.

Ginger sat aisle side, saving a spot for Basil. She smiled down at Scout, who looked small and bored seated between her and Ambrosia. Scout was the reason Ginger and Oliver had become acquainted, as meeting Scout on the SS *Rosa* had inspired Ginger to start a food programme for street children. She and Oliver then started the Child Wellness programme which continued to serve meals to the less fortunate.

As was tradition, the bride's family and friends sat on one side, the groom's on the other. Though the Gold family and friends were new to London, they were an established line from Hertfordshire. Likewise, the Hartigan family, Ginger's parents and ancestors, was well established. And even though Charles' parents had now passed away, and he an only child, an earl from anywhere in England had long-running extended family lines.

Ginger scanned the faces across the aisle in a covert way—adjusting her hat, checking her watch, moving her handbag, and removing a handkerchief. All small movements considered normal in the circumstances that would not draw attention.

She was looking for the names she'd recognised on the guest list that had caused her alarm. Jean-Claude Beaulieu, Pierre Dubois, Harry Webster.

When she'd spotted them, her gaze stayed for a split second. Jean-Claude and Mr. Webster were much as she remembered them, only older. The first tall and angular with a sharp jawline and pointing elbows, and the latter with a flattened nose as if it were once broken and left to heal without medical attention. A blonde lady sat closely with Jean-Claude, a wife.

Mr. Dubois alone didn't have a place in the pew but sat in a wheelchair at the back of the nave. His brown hair was parted to one side, and an angry-looking scar on his left cheek seemed to be high-lighted by sun rays coming from the church windows.

Staring blankly ahead, Ginger considered the possibilities. She'd been astounded to see his name on the list in the first place, as she'd known he'd been disabled in the Great War. Ginger felt a wave of sympathy. So many had given up so much, but thankfully everyone's effort wasn't for naught. The allies had won the war to end all wars, and Mr. Dubois' sacrifice had been worth it.

And Daniel's.

Ginger shook off the melancholy that threatened to captivate her. Those were sad days, but they were over. She ran a hand over her rounded stomach. New life and new hope were to come.

Charles exited the vestry along with his best man, his good friend Mr. Hughes, and stood in front of the pulpit facing the congregation. The church organ, situated high on the balcony at the back of the church, came to life, the organist pounding on the keys, starting the bridal march.

The congregation stood, waiting in anticipation for their first view of the bride. In all the time that Ginger had known Charles Davenport-Witt, she'd never seen him radiate nerves, and yet she could see the intensity of this moment in his dark eyes.

Since Felicia was fatherless, Basil took the role of walking the bride down the aisle. Felicia was stunning in her white gown, and even with the veil covering her face, one could sense her happiness and see a glimpse of a smile.

Basil, so handsome in his single-breasted morning coat, gold cufflinks peeking out from the sleeves, made Ginger's heart race. How fortunate was she to have a man like that to call her husband!

Behind them came a flock of little girls dressed in frilly white dresses and carrying small baskets. They were followed by the bridesmaids dressed in flapper-style dresses with netted caps on their heads and holding enormous floral bouquets.

Basil remained with Felicia when they reached the front, but from the way the young couple's eyes stayed on each other, Ginger could tell that no one else in the church mattered to either of them.

Oliver stepped behind the pulpit. Over his black cassock, he wore a white surplice and silk embroidered stole. He opened his arms and greeted the congregation.

"Dearly beloved, we are gathered together here in the sight of God, and in the face of this congregation, to join together this man and this woman in Holy Matrimony."

As if the entire congregation had been holding its breath, at least on the bride's side, a collective sense of relief settled on the guests. Felicia and Charles were here, faces bright with excitement and anticipation, and nothing untoward had prevented their imminent happiness. Ambrosia seemed to burst with joy; a showing Ginger had rarely witnessed.

"This is an honourable estate, instituted of God in the time of man's innocence, signifying unto us the mystical union that is betwixt Christ and his Church; which holy estate Christ adorned and beautified with his presence, and the first miracle that he wrought, in Cana of Galilee; and is commended of Saint Paul to be honourable among all men—"

Oliver flipped a page, then continued, "and therefore is not by any to be enterprised, nor taken in hand, unadvisedly, lightly, or wantonly, to satisfy men's carnal lusts and appetites, like brute beasts—"

A casual glance over Ginger's shoulder showed her young maids at the back pressing gloved fingers against their mouths to hold in their giggles at the imagery. Mrs. Beasley's stern look quickly brought them into order.

"—that do not understand; but reverently, discreetly, advisedly, soberly, and in the fear of God; duly considering the causes for which Matrimony was ordained."

Ginger cast Basil a smile of amusement.

"First, it was ordained for the procreation of children, to be brought up in the fear and nurture of the Lord, and to the praise of His holy Name.

"Second, it was ordained for a remedy against sin, and to avoid fornication; that such persons as have not the gift of continency might marry and keep themselves undefiled members of Christ's body."

At this, a bout of coughing came from one of Felicia's bridesmaids. She blushed as if horrified; Felicia shot her a scathing look. Oliver smoothly continued as if nothing were amiss.

"Third, it was ordained for the mutual society, help, and comfort, that the one ought to have of the other, both in prosperity and adversity. Into which holy estate these two persons present come now to be joined."

The way Charles gazed at Felicia with eyes filled with pride and affection, Ginger chastised herself for ever being worried.

"Therefore," Oliver went on, "if any man can shew just cause, why they may not lawfully be joined together, let him now speak, or else forever hold his peace."

A moment of quiet passed as everyone held their breath, and then Oliver started, "I require and charge—"

"I object!"

A collective gasp was followed by the sounds of frocks and suits shifting in the pews as necks turned.

A brunette woman with fiery eyes stood with an accusing finger pointed at the groom. "That man is not who he says he is." Her voice, shaking and foreign, echoed through the nave. "His name is *Henri Pomeroy.* We were lovers in Belgium. He is not a real earl. He is only interested in this lady's money!"

Ginger felt as if someone had plunked down on her chest. She stared at the accuser then swivelled to find Felicia, who'd grown very pale.

Basil shot Ginger a disconcerting glance and she could almost read his mind. *What the deuce is going on?*

Oliver took charge. "Please, everyone. Calm yourselves. I can attest to the identification of the man who stands before you. I've seen legitimate documentation that proves that this man is the Earl of Witt, and this church is filled with people who can testify to that."

Basil left his spot to tend to the distraught interloper. Constable Braxton helped to escort her out.

Ambrosia gripped Ginger's arm. "Dear Lord! Good thing there are no newspaper men inside the church."

Trust Grandmother to be more concerned about reputation than how tormenting this interruption must be for her granddaughter.

A crimson blush of embarrassment had replaced

Felicia's pale complexion. She glared at Charles, who shook his head. He whispered something in Felicia's ear that appeared to appease her. She forced a smile, which she directed at the guests.

Having experienced handling many kinds of awkward situations, Oliver brought everyone's focus back to the happy couple and the nuptials at hand.

Ginger's focus was on Charles, and when, for a split second, he caught her gaze, her heart pounded.

She wasn't the only one in the church who believed the brunette with the French accent. She, along with Harry Webster, Jean-Claude Beaulieu, and Pierre Dubois had known Henri Pomeroy. It had been one of Charles' many aliases.

Oh mercy!

CHAPTER FOUR

Ginger caught Felicia's eye with a questioning look of her own. Was she all right? Would she continue with the ceremony?

Felicia's eyelashes fluttered as she gave Ginger a subtle nod. The wedding would proceed. Ginger wished she had enhanced hearing—what she would give to know what Charles had spoken in Felicia's ear to reassure her.

The couple turned to Oliver, who, as if a disturbance hadn't even occurred, continued in his much-needed comforting manner, though a moment of awkwardness ensued as Basil hurried back to his place at Felicia's side.

Looking at Charles, Oliver recited, "Wilt thou

have this woman to thy wedded wife, to live together after God's ordinance in the holy estate of Matrimony? Wilt thou love her, comfort her, honour, and keep her, in sickness and in health; and, forsaking all others, keep thee only unto her, so long as ye both shall live?"

Charles, his eyes on Felicia, replied, "I will."

Oliver repeated the question to Felicia, and she too, responded, "I will."

To Basil, Oliver asked, "Who giveth this woman to be married to this man?"

Basil answered, "I do."

Oliver, as tradition held, took Felicia by her left hand, and handed her over to Charles who reached for her with his right. Basil slipped away, taking the seat Ginger had saved for him.

It was Charles' turn to declare his vow. "I Charles Davenport-Witt, the Earl of Witt, take thee Felicia Gold to be my wedded wife, to have and to hold from this day forward, for better for worse, for richer or for poorer, in sickness and in health, to love and to cherish, till death us do part, according to God's holy ordinance; and thereto I plight thee my troth."

Ginger's eyes were good and truly damp by the time Felicia repeated her vows and the rings were exchanged. When Oliver pronounced the couple married, Ginger reached across Scout to take Ambrosia's bony hand and smiled. Ambrosia wasn't one to openly express tender emotion, but Ginger was certain she saw happy tears well up in the matriarchs hooded eyes.

After the ceremony, the newlyweds stepped outside and faced the cheering crowd. Felicia's bridesmaids were a flash of colour amongst the autumn-brown and black coats with fur-trimmed collars. The organ played loudly and could be heard outside as well-wishers threw rice. Ginger thought it best to get the bridal party out of the cool breeze before they froze to death.

It was a slow caravan of motorcars that finally broke through the mass of onlookers, driving to Belgravia and Charles' grand house on Wilton Crescent.

Even from the street, with only a view of the short side of the house, the Davenport-Witt family residence known as Witt House was an impressive limestone structure four storeys high. Felicia had given Ginger the grand tour on a previous visit, hardly able to contain her glee at becoming the lady of such a spectacular house.

The pillared entrance opened to the corridor on the ground level. On the left was a cloakroom for hanging coats and hats, and on the right, French doors led to a sitting room, which opened into a smaller vestibule, a morning room, with doors that opened to the back garden. At the end of the corridor was a study that also had doors opening to the garden.

By the front entrance, a set of cement steps led to the basement level where the kitchen and eating area for the servants was situated.

Ginger and her party were escorted up the staircase to the first floor, where the wedding party was taking place in the ballroom. The attached drawing room was used for receiving guests and for those who'd rather mingle than dance—and in this instance, used for a luncheon buffet—and beyond, a lovely stone terrace looked down on the garden.

Overnight guests were put up in bedrooms on the third floor, above the master suite which took up the entire second floor. There was also a separate guest house—a converted stable—besides the garage at the back of the garden.

If Ginger hadn't loved Hartigan House so much, she might've been envious.

The ballroom was filled with wedding guests, many sitting in chairs along the perimeter, including the two widows from Mallowan Court, Mrs. Schofield and Lady Whitmore. Ginger stopped to greet each one, both looking exhausted by the affair already, even though it was only the middle of the afternoon.

"Lovely house," Mrs. Schofield said. "I imagine Ambrosia will want to move in with her granddaughter now, not that there's anything wrong with Hartigan House."

Ginger bit her cheek to keep herself from blurting out how Hartigan House was a step above the Schofield residence, and held her tongue. "I believe Felicia and I will have to fight over Ambrosia, as I'm not quite ready to give her up."

Rather more cultured, but even less reserved than Mrs. Schofield, Lady Whitmore said, "I'm thrilled for the new Lady Davenport-Witt. This house will keep her occupied, I expect. I've heard there's been a large turn-over in staff over the years."

Ginger kept herself from frowning at the lady, a known gossip in London circles. "I'm certain that will change once a lady of the manor is in charge."

She excused herself and stopped to greet other members of their society. She was thankful she'd brought a fan along to breeze herself, as the space was already overly warm, despite the windows having been opened.

A table with two chairs was set up for the bride and groom, and Felicia and Charles drank wine and talked animatedly to their guests. Even from her spot across the room, Ginger could see that Felicia was deliriously happy and the unfortunate scene at the church forgotten.

At least for now.

Several tables with white cloths and floral centrepieces lined the edge of the room, and after finding the one assigned to them, near the new couple, Basil and Scout left to find beverages.

Ambrosia sat beside Ginger, her eyes on the newly wedded couple, and sighed.

"What's the matter, Grandmother?" Ginger asked lightly. "Your heart's desire has come to pass."

"Yes, I know. I'm delighted for Felicia, and relieved, frankly, to cross the item off my list. She is his concern now. I'm far too old to manage that kind of youthful energy."

Ginger empathised. Ambrosia had had to play the role of mother twice, first with her son Robert, then when he and his wife died, her grandson and granddaughter. It hadn't been easy, bringing up Felicia, who'd proved to be a wild child. She had been raised without a father, and her only sibling, Ginger's late husband, Daniel, had died at the end of the war when Felicia was still a child. Ginger thought Felicia had come around nicely, despite these hardships.

Ambrosia's shoulders dropped. "Felicia's felicity brings the Gold name to an end."

Ginger glanced at the older lady kindly. Though Ginger and Daniel had wanted a family, a child had failed to materialise, and then it was too late.

However, the Gold name had ended before that. It was a family secret Ambrosia had kept and only shared under duress after a tragedy at the Royal Albert Hall. A secret Ginger had promised to keep.

"I'm going to go and say hello to the happy couple," Ginger said. "Before the dancing starts. Would you like to come with me?"

"I spoke to her at the church." Ambrosia leaned against her walking stick and held in a yawn. "I'll wait here."

Ginger lowered her shawl, so it hung loosely around her hips and carried her handbag as a barrier in front of her. Even so, it was hard to maintain her graceful gait with the extra weight she carried, but fortunately, everyone's attention was on the bride and groom.

"Oh, Ginger!" Felicia said when she spotted her. Felicia excused herself from her adoring guests and gripped Ginger's gloved hands. "Oh, Ginger, can you believe it? I'm a married lady!"

"Indeed you are, *Lady Davenport-Witt!*"

Felicia squealed with rapture at her new handle. "That sounds so heavenly! Charles and I are going to have the best lives together; I just know it. I'm the luckiest lady in the world!"

Ginger delighted in Felicia's joy. She kissed her on the cheek. "I do wish you many happy years together, darling. You're all right with what happened—"

She left the prying statement hanging, hoping Felicia would finish it without feeling offence.

Felicia's expression fell, and Ginger felt remorse for bringing up the insensitive subject. Whatever it was that Charles had told Felicia, was moot now, since the nuptials were over. "She's from his past," Felicia whispered. "And clearly unhinged." She smiled appealingly at Ginger. "And it really doesn't matter now. What matters is that Charles is mine and I am his."

"You're absolutely right," Ginger said with

conviction. "And you both deserve all the happiness in the world."

"Thank you, Ginger."

Ginger took a step back as Charles approached. He placed Felicia's hand in his and nodded. "Ginger."

"Congratulations, Charles. You've made Felicia an incredibly happy blushing bride."

Charles gazed at Felicia with eyes filled with affection. "I'm the luckiest of men."

Seeing them together, so in love, caused Ginger to chastise herself for ever calling this union into question. Charles was a mature, capable man, and Felicia was in good hands.

"Charles, old chap!" A man approached their small grouping and patted Charles on the back. He reached out a hand to Ginger and continued in his melodious Welsh accent, "Mrs. Reed. Such a splendid affair, is it not?"

Ginger recognised Maximillian Hughes, a good college chum of Charles whom she'd met before. A confirmed bachelor, at least up to now, the Welshman had a pleasant face with a high-ridged nose and eyes that looked glassy with drink.

"Mr. Hughes. Such a pleasure to see you again."

"Thank you, Mrs. Reed." He patted Charles on

the back again. "Davenport-Witt and I go way back. I'm honoured to be his best man."

"The honour is mine, old chap," Charles said, patting Mr. Hughes back.

"Thrilled for you!" A third pat on the back convinced Ginger that Mr. Hughes had spent some time imbibing from the bar. He continued, "Charles is the best mate a man could ask for, but today is about you, mate," he said, with a fourth pat on the back. Someone called his name, and he spun on his heel and walked away.

"How's your back, Charles?" Ginger asked playfully.

Charles made a show of rolling his shoulders. "Very close to being put out, I'd say. Good thing he was called away." He fished out a pocket watch from his waistcoat pocket.

"Eager to get going, are you?" Ginger said with a tease.

"I'll readily admit to that."

"You must delight us by dancing with your bride before you leave."

"We'll have you sent off in plenty of time," Ginger said. "But you must delight us by dancing with your bride before you leave."

The band comprising brass instruments, a

double bass, and a small drum kit announced they would soon begin, and Ginger returned to her place next to Ambrosia. Soon the dance floor was filled with couples waltzing to the music of Eric Coates. Ginger loved to dance, but hiding one's girth was hard enough when sitting, much less dancing. Regretfully, she'd have to sit this out today and instead find joy in watching others—many socialites she had become acquainted with since her return to London—on the dance floor.

Ginger recognised some couples and watched fondly. Madame Roux, the manager of Ginger's dress shop, Feathers & Flair, danced with Inspector Sanders, a Father-Christmas type of fellow with sparkling blue eyes. Ginger had known the unlikely pair would be here—her at Ginger's invitation and him at Basil's. Not normally part of this upper-class crowd, they kept to the sidelines when not dancing. Though Inspector Sanders was clearly taken with his dance partner, his gaze moved about the room, staying aware of his professional capacity. Ginger appreciated that.

Felicia's bridesmaids were the life of the party, dancing with every available single gentleman—and some not so single—their raucous laughter growing louder with each cocktail. Ginger hoped Felicia wouldn't miss the carefree lifestyle she'd enjoyed with her single female friends. In time, each would likely marry, though the bachelor to maiden ratio had been skewed to the bachelor's favour since the war.

Constable Newman stood near the drinks table, a fine place to observe and overhear a potentially troubling conversation. At the door, Constable Braxton, poor thing, could not keep his eyes off Felicia. She had teased him with a show of mild affection but had moved on as social requirements had dictated. Basil had reassured her that Constable Braxton had his choice of fair maidens and to not to fret over the condition of the young man's heart.

Ginger hoped she was worrying over the evening for nothing. Later, she and Basil would discuss the lovely time they had had as they cuddled together in their bed. She blamed her excessive nerves on her situation. Oliver's wife, Matilda, who'd once been a medical student and now helped midwives, had warned her about hormones that made one more sensitive than usual and not to be alarmed by unexpected bouts of emotion.

"What did we miss?" Basil said jovially as he and Scout returned to where Ginger sat.

"Just the dancing," Ginger said, feigning a pout. Basil took her hand.

"We'll be on the dance floor again once our little one is here," he said kindly. "I promise."

Ginger patted his arm. "Well, you mustn't miss out on the fun on my account. Felicia has plenty of lady friends waiting to be asked to dance—" Ginger nodded to her shop manager. "And Madame Roux, when Inspector Sanders, needs a rest."

Basil studied the inspector as he danced, then stared at Constables Braxton and Newman. He gave Ginger an encouraging look.

"I suppose you're right, love." Basil stood and offered his hand to the dowager. "Lady Gold, would you do me the honour?"

Ambrosia blustered. "I don't think—"

"Oh, do go, Grandmother," Ginger said. "Before the waltzing music ends. You must put Basil out of his misery."

"Very well." Ambrosia leaned on the silver handle of her walking stick. "If you don't mind this object in the way."

"Not at all," Basil said.

Ginger beamed as she watched her husband walk with Ambrosia to an open space on the floor, then taking her crooked, ring-adorned hands in his and leading her in a gentle sway.

"When can we go?" Scout asked. He might be

moving out of the stage where he found girls disgusting, but he wasn't ready to take on dancing with any of them.

"We must wait for the bride and groom to depart," Ginger said. She was fatigued enough to go home in time for dinner, though many guests would happily party into the night at Charles' expense. "Why don't you find another piece of cake."

Finding herself alone at the table, Ginger sipped her tea. Her eye caught Jean-Claude Beaulieu as he danced with the lady he'd come with. Ginger didn't know if she was his wife or girlfriend. If there was a ring, it was hidden by the lady's gloves, but the way they held their bodies together, they were definitely more than friends.

The music ended, and Basil led Ambrosia out of the ballroom, perhaps to find the powder room, as the younger crowd danced the Charleston. Felicia and Charles were surprisingly good together—both kicking their heels back and to the side as their arms flung in the opposite direction. The crowd pushed back to watch as the newlyweds took the centre spot. Though Ginger couldn't dance at that moment, it didn't stop her feet from tapping. She held her long strand of beads in one hand and twirled them.

So enthralled was she that she didn't notice she

was being watched until her chair was bumped, and her drink swished near the lip of the glass. Her head snapped back, and she gaped at Pierre Dubois, who'd rolled his wheelchair over to her.

"*Pardon, madame,*" he said, his accent strongly French. "Zees contraptions are not exactly roadworthy."

"Hello," Ginger said, surprised. She'd remembered him, of course, but she hadn't expected to be recognised in return. Certainly, her red hair didn't help, but she'd worn it long in those days, usually in braids, and she never wore makeup. As far as Monsieur Dubois and Charles' other French companions were concerned, Ginger had been thoroughly French and had no reason to be at this wedding.

With a crisp English accent, she said, "I'm afraid these places are taken."

"I would not dream of usurping, *madame.*"

Ginger nodded and looked away, hoping if she ignored him, he'd leave her.

Pierre Dubois didn't take her hint. "I could dance well," he said. "*Tres bien.* Before zee war."

Ginger offered him a consoling glance. "The war was a horrible time. My first husband died while I waited for him in America."

"America?" Monsieur Dubois said with a note of amusement. "I have not had zee opportunity to go. What ees it like?"

She tried not to stare at the scar cut deep into his cheek in the shape of a "Y." "It's everything you'd imagine it would be, Mr.—"

"Dubois."

"A bit wild and untamed. Zealous. Hopeful. Not weighted down by centuries of history like we are here."

"Was your husband American?"

"No. English. But, at his insistence and for my safety, I stayed with my American family."

"Very sensible."

The music ended, and the tired and happy dancers dispersed. Ginger hoped that meant the end of these forced niceties, and was expecting Mr. Dubois to move on. Sadly, it wasn't to be. He startled her by asking, "How is our friend, Antoinette?"

Ginger kept her expression blank. "I'm afraid I don't know who you mean."

Thankfully, Harry Webster spotted them and stumbled over as one does when one has had too much to drink.

"Pierre! There you are, you old dog!" He grabbed the handles of Mr. Dubois' chair, but instead of taking his friend away, his eyes narrowed as they latched on Ginger. "Hidee ho, fair maiden. How tragic that you're not dancing."

Ginger forced a smile. "I'm not a maiden, I'm afraid." She moved her fan that had shielded the evidence beneath it.

Mr. Webster snorted. "Clearly not, madam."

Mr. Dubois twisted to stare at his friend. "Webster, must you always be an impudent swine?"

"My apologies." Mr. Webster straightened, catching a belch with his fist. "Now, let us be on our way."

Fire flashed behind Mr. Dubois' eye as he became captive to the whims of his friend, unable to stop him without creating a scene.

Ginger felt empathy for the man but was grateful to be out of his insightful interrogation.

Basil returned with Ambrosia that moment, and she settled in as gracefully as one could at her age. "I'm sorry to hold on to your husband for so long, Ginger, but nature called, and I wasn't sure I'd find my way back on my own.

Basil stared at Ginger with a furrowed brow. He leaned in and whispered. "Is everything all right? You look shaken."

Ginger inhaled calmly. She'd lost her edge since

the war, which had been made clear often, but she hoped Basil could read her emotions because he knew her so well and not because she'd failed utterly to control them.

"Just missed you," she said. Her eyes darted to Pierre Dubois, who was once again in position across the room. He knew who she was, but after all this time, did it matter? She was compelled by secrecy, but the French government demanded it of him as well.

Scout ran to the table, a plate with a piece of cake on it in hand, and Ginger realised she hadn't even thought about her son's whereabouts since Mr. Dubois had banged into the table. What a terrible mother she had been! She ran a hand over her belly, feeling a moment of insecurity. This feeling, too, Matilda had promised her, would pass in time.

"Scout, love, come sit by me," she said. She patted his shoulder, as he did what she had bid, more to comfort herself than for his sake.

CHAPTER FIVE

"Darling," Ginger said warmly, "I think it's my turn to visit the powder room. I assume it can be found in the corridor?"

"Indeed," Basil said. "Would you like me to accompany you as well?"

Ginger chuckled. "I think I can manage. You stay here with Ambrosia and Scout."

Like many houses on Wilton Crescent, Witt House had a bathroom on each floor. Ginger found the one on the first floor unoccupied and took possession. Once she'd completed her business, she washed her hands in the basin and studied her reflection in the mirror. Her hair was short to the bottom of her ears, and the marcel waves Lizzie had hot-ironed in held nicely. Her eyebrows were plucked in wide, thin arches, so unlike their natural state during the war, thick and straight. Blue eyeshadow made her green eyes look deeper and larger, and her lips were painted rosebud-red. How on earth had Pierre Dubois recognised her from the simple and plain-looking girl from the war?

She supposed that was what had made him such a brilliant spy.

Harry Webster and Jean-Claude Beaulieu were equally good and perhaps more subtle. Harry's drunken performance could quite likely have been just that, a performance, and if Ginger wasn't mistaken, Mr. Beaulieu had glanced in her direction more than would be deemed normal.

Ginger shook her shoulders. She had to get herself together. None of it mattered. She was only being affected by their presence at the wedding because of the memories seeing them again had stirred up.

Just as Ginger unlocked the bathroom door, it swung open, and she nearly ran into the blonde, Jean-Claude Beaulieu's guest.

"Hello!" she said chipperly. "Bride or groom?" She laughed as if her question was hilarious. Her accent was clearly English.

"Bride," Ginger returned.

"Groom here." She leaned in to glimpse her reflection in the mirror. "I don't know him from Adam. According to my gentleman friend, Jean-Claude—" The lady opened a small handbag and removed a powder compact. She motioned for Ginger to stay as she patted her nose. "They served together in the Great War. He never talked about Lord Davenport-Witt, so I was surprised when he said he was coming to London to go to his wedding."

Ginger hovered in the doorway. "How did you and Mr. Jean-Claude—"

"*Beaulieu.* So French, isn't it? Just rolls of one's tongue. *Beaulieu.*"

"Indeed," Ginger said. "How did you and Mr. Beaulieu meet?"

The blonde smiled, flashing her big white teeth. "At a club in Paris. There's nothing like it here in London." She held out her hand. "I'm Olivia Ward, by the way."

Ginger shook Miss Ward's hand. "I'm Ginger Reed. I'm here with my husband and son. The bride is the sister of my late husband."

"Married twice, eh? I'm still waiting for my first go-around. I'm hoping this wedding has given Jean-Claude ideas! Anyway—" She motioned to the toilet. "I do have to—"

"Of course," Ginger said. "It was nice to meet you, Miss Ward."

"Likewise." She wiggled her fingers. "Toodle-oo!"

As Ginger headed back to the ballroom, she was overcome with a wave of fatigue. Checking her watch, she wondered how long before Felicia and Charles left for the Ritz where they intended to spend the first night of their married life?

Basil enjoyed a good party as well as the next fellow, but he was coming to the end of this afternoon. Ambrosia and Scout appeared as if they were washed out and fading as well.

"Would you like to be taken home?" he asked Ambrosia.

"I would, but it's too soon for you and Ginger to be leaving," she said. "Felicia would never forgive you. However, when one gets to be my age, one can get away with things one couldn't in one's youth."

"Shall I ring for Clement?"

"If you would," Ambrosia said. "In the meantime, I'll say goodbye to the happy couple." She glanced at Scout without smiling. "You might as well come too."

Ambrosia had had a challenging time accepting a "street urchin" into the family, but in time, and as Scout shed the evidence of his unfortunate beginnings, she made slight allowances like this one.

"Dad?" Scout said, having never been invited to do anything by the family matriarch.

"Go and say goodbye to Aunt Felicia and Lord Charles." Aunt Felicia and Lord Charles were the agreed names they had assigned for Scout's benefit. "Then you can go home to Boss with Lady Gold."

Scout sauntered off, satisfied with the arrangement.

Basil arranged for a staff member to ring Hartigan House. As he waited for Ginger to return, he approached his young constable, who was still in the guise of a footman.

"Braxton."

The constable straightened at Basil's voice. "Sir. It was a lovely wedding, sir."

"Nothing of concern noted?"

"No, sir. Just the usual poor behaviour that comes with too much drink. Newman and I steered the guilty parties to the terrace for fresh air."

"Good enough," Basil said.

Braxton's gaze darted back to the queen of the ball, the new Lady Davenport-Witt, and his puppy-dog eyes nearly stared forlornly. Basil gave him a sharp pat on the back.

"She was always meant for someone like the earl, Braxton. Buckle up. Stiff upper lip and all that. You'll find the proper girl for you in no time."

Streaks of red rushed up Braxton's neck. "Yes, sir."

"Weren't you stepping out with that model?"

"Miss Tatum?"

"Yes, her, from the fashion show debacle in Hyde Park. She models for Ginger at her shop."

Braxton nodded once. "We've gone out a few times. I think I'll ring her up tomorrow, see if she'll go to the pictures with me."

"Good idea."

"Do you want us to stick around, sir, or take off?"

Basil was about to release his men, but something stopped him. Ginger had asked for the detail, and though it appeared her concerns were unmerited, the day wasn't over, and Basil had learned to take his wife's instincts seriously.

"Stick around for a bit, if you don't mind."

The population of the ballroom had thinned considerably. Sanders sat by himself, and Basil took a jaunt his way.

"Oh, 'ello, Chief Inspector," Sanders said. "Grand 'ol party, init?"

"Indeed." Basil lowered himself into a chair and loosened his tie.

"I appreciated the invitation and got to spend time wiv me girl—" he chuckled. "Now don't let 'er know I call 'er that! She'd 'ave me 'ead, but what was the 'ullabaloo about?"

"No hullabaloo, Sanders, just a bit of precaution. The earl's a pretty important bloke."

"Oh, I see, sir. Glad to be of service to protect the likes of 'im."

Basil watched the few revellers left on the dance floor, tipsy partners leaning on each other as the band played. Ambrosia and Felicia embraced, Felicia's exuberance overwhelming her grandmother, who stiffened even as she reciprocated. Scout waved as he and Ambrosia exited the room. Basil wasn't sure that Ambrosia could remember how to find the front door, as the house was a bit of a labyrinth, but Scout would find the way just fine and assist Ambrosia with the stairs. He turned back to Sanders.

"Madame Roux is having an enjoyable time, I hope?"

"Yeah, she is." Sanders' blue eyes flashed. "I'm a fine dancer, I'll 'ave you know."

Basil felt his lips twitch. "I never doubted it. If you don't mind keeping watch a little longer, I'd appreciate it."

"Certainly, Chief Inspector."

Basil caught sight of Ginger as she stepped back into the room. He felt his cheeks tighten as his lips pulled into an involuntary smile. He still couldn't believe that he'd landed a lady like Ginger, and as he'd vowed on their wedding day, he'd never taken one day with her for granted. She was everything he'd dreamed of: beautiful, sophisticated, intelligent, open yet mysterious, gentle and yet strong, and a joy to spend time with. She made him laugh, think, and often change his mind. Her hand went to her growing stomach, and Basil's love for her seemed to multiply at that moment. She carried his child, an experience he'd once believed was never to be his to enjoy.

She smiled when she caught sight of him, her green eyes flashing with fondness. He jumped to his feet to go to her.

But before he reached her, he was intercepted by Charles' best man, Hughes.

"Chief Inspector Reed," Hughes said, rolling the "R" in his surname, his voice as loose as the amber fluid in his glass. Whisky, Basil guessed, by its lighter tone.

"I was hoping for a few moments with you before the night is through," Hughes continued. Basil cast a glance beyond the man and flashed a look of apology Ginger's way. She waved him off and sat at their table.

"How can I be of service?"

"A fabulous wedding, eh? Davenport-Witt has never been happier. I've known him for a long time and can attest to that."

"That's very good to hear."

Hughes rubbed his pointy chin. "I couldn't help but notice you had men at the doors. Superb job, having them out of uniform, but I have to say, I can smell a copper a mile away." He grinned. "No offence. Just a gift of intuition."

Basil eyed the man. From his experience, that sort of gift of intuition came from a familiarity with the law, and more precisely, familiarity with breaking the law.

"I'm sure you're mistaken," Basil said coyly. "Why would I have reason to add law enforcement to this gathering of London's finest citizens?"

"Yes, that was my question as well, Chief Inspector." He gestured with a flourish. "But as you can see, there is nothing unexpected going on here." Hughes headed across the ballroom in a crooked line as if he were dodging invisible dancers.

"That looked like an intense conversation," Ginger said when Basil reached her. "Like everyone beside you and me, it seems, the man has had a bit too much to drink. Good thing he's an overnight guest."

Felicia and Charles were preparing to leave, saying goodbye to the guests who'd gathered around. He was certain they were eager to begin their wedding journey. He and Ginger joined them, saying farewell with kisses on the cheeks and slaps on the back.

Felicia wiped tears away from under her eyes, then clasped Ginger's hand.

"I'll see you in a few weeks, love," Ginger said.

"Both as married ladies now," Felicia gushed, unable to rein in her characteristic childishness. Basil gathered, with Charles at her side and the responsibilities that came with being the wife of an important figure such as an earl, that Felicia's wild days of being a "bright young thing," would come to a crashing end. Yet, Basil hoped she'd have a good wedding journey with many pleasant memories to hold her through the tougher times which were sure to come.

"You'll love Greece," Ginger said, "and come home with a lovely, sun-kissed glow."

Once the wedding couple departed, the guests began to take their leave as well, until just a few remnants remained. Basil had suggested that they depart as well, but Ginger insisted, that they remain in lieu of Felicia and Charles as the wedding hosts. It was still only late afternoon, after all.

The band leader announced the last dance, a waltz, and Basil reached out his hand. "Mrs. Reed, might you do me the honour?"

"In my condition?" Ginger teased.

"I'll hold you up, I promise. Just this one. It's a slow dance. You'll barely be moving at all."

Basil let out a contented sigh as he held his wife close and turned her slowly about the dance floor. Basil leaned back and held Ginger's gaze.

"The only thing that never changes is that everything always changes," she said.

"So true."

"Felicia will leave a hole at Hartigan House."

"Our little one will do more than fill it."

"Yes, you're right. And like you said, Felicia is only just across town. She's not leaving the country."

"I suspect you'll see even more of each other, from desperately missing one another so."

"I do hope you're right."

When Basil finally pulled his gaze away from his wife's face, he was surprised to find they were the last on the floor. He and Ginger continued to sway to the music, honouring the band. When the music ended, the bandleader announced, "That's it for us this afternoon. Thank you to the bride and groom for allowing us to be a part of their special day."

Those who remained offered applause of gratitude, the sound followed by a gunshot.

CHAPTER SIX

Ginger cast a glance at Basil. "Please tell me that was the sound of a motorcar backfiring!" Even as the words left her mouth, Ginger knew her hope was in vain. Wilton Crescent ran along the front of the house, but even if one motorcar had backfired, they wouldn't have heard it in the ballroom, especially not that loudly.

Basil shouted to his constables, "Seal the doors, men. Don't let anyone leave!" To Ginger, he said, "Stay here."

Normally, Ginger would bristle at being told to stay behind on an investigation, but in her present physical condition, she could hardly disagree.

"Please do hurry back," she said. A brief time

later Basil returned, and by the sombre look on his face Ginger knew the news would not be good.

"Basil?"

"I'm afraid Mr. Beaulieu has been fatally wounded."

Ginger's heart sunk. "Mr. Beaulieu?" One of Charles' friends from France. She'd been right to be concerned, but unfortunately, her caution hadn't prevented a death.

"Braxton and Newman are at the scene," Basil said. "Sanders is routing everyone who hadn't yet left the house and who was also not in the ballroom when the pistol went off to the sitting room."

"I presume it's safe to have a look?" Ginger said.

Basil held out his arm, and Ginger linked hers with his, saying, "Let's do what we must."

THE BACK GARDEN was a well-manicured affair with trimmed hedges, flower beds planted strategically, and a Y-shaped flagstone path that led from the guest house and garage to both rear entrances of the house: the study and the morning room. A three-tiered cement fountain, turned off for the season, was in the middle of the Y, and on either side, the gardeners had placed ornate wrought-iron benches for one to enjoy the garden while seated, perhaps reading.

The body of Mr. Beaulieu lay face down on the grassy surface between the fountain and the guesthouse, rumpled awkwardly with a circle of red on the upper left side of his back, his blood seeping into the earth.

It appeared the bullet had gone straight through his heart.

Basil sought his constables. "Braxton?"

"Sir. We're searching the grounds for the bullet and weapon."

"And the pathologist has been called?"

"Yes, sir. Inspector Sanders said he'd ring him up."

"Witnesses?"

"None that have come forward, sir."

The back garden was not easily accessed if one didn't know the house. The exit doors led from the extended sitting room and the study and not from the end of the corridor, as one might assume. Ginger wondered what had drawn Mr. Beaulieu down to the garden, a level below the ballroom. If one desired fresh air, one could simply access the terrace situated off the back of the reception room, off the ballroom. One might cut through to access the guest house—

Mr. Webster and Mr. Dubois were staying in the rooms there—but Mr. Beaulieu was not an overnight guest.

Ginger supposed one could accidentally happen upon it if one had been tempted to wander about the house without invitation.

For two people to happen upon it individually, and one with murderous intentions? No, the odds were too great. Though two could've found their way here by accident, with one sensing an opportunity.

"Where is Miss Ward?" Ginger asked.

"Who?" Basil said.

"Olivia Ward, Mr. Beaulieu's date?"

Constable Braxton checked his notepad, then answered. "She's with Inspector Sanders in the sitting room."

In most other cases where a body is discovered, there is time spent waiting for the police to arrive, but since Ginger had made a request for police presence beforehand, officers were already on site.

"How did you know?" Basil asked.

Ginger, who'd found a place to rest on one of the benches, functional if not comfortable, turned to her husband's voice. He stood to her side and watched her.

"Know what, love?" she returned.

"That extra security was needed tonight?" He nodded toward the body. "Not that it helped that man."

Ginger looked away. "Just a hunch."

Basil tugged on his trousers as he took a seat beside her. He shifted his weight and said, "Frightfully uncomfortable."

"Quite, but there's little option out here." Ginger wrapped her shawl more tightly around her shoulders. "And not exactly a summer's evening."

Basil wrapped an arm around her. "Let me be of service."

Ginger snuggled in. "Oh, that's much better."

"Yes. Now, don't think for a moment I've forgotten my question."

"What question?"

"How did you know that there would be trouble tonight?"

"I didn't know."

"But you suspected, otherwise, my men would be on their way here instead of having been here for hours already."

Ginger pinched her eyes as she let out a breath. This was the very thing she had wanted to shield Felicia from—awkward conversations cornering Charles into a lie.

She went with a half-truth. "I recalled reading, years ago, about a Monsieur Beaulieu, who'd been suspected of fraud. It was during my time as a telephone operator in France. I don't know why I remembered that event, it was so long ago, but I worried about his presence at Felicia's wedding." She patted her stomach. "Matilda says it's normal to become overly protective and emotional over those you love during this time in a lady's life."

"I see," Basil said. "And what a coincidence that you happened to be right and not merely emotional."

"A dreadfully sad coincidence, indeed. However," Ginger jumped at the chance to change the subject. "Though I hate to bring bad news to Felicia and Charles on their wedding night, they really must be informed."

"I'll see that a call is made to the hotel," Basil said, "but I don't see a reason for them to be questioned or for Charles to return here tonight."

Ginger exhaled. "That's a relief."

"Sir?" Constable Braxton interrupted. "I have the bullet, sir." He held it out with a gloved hand. "A .445 calibre. I've put a marker on the ground where I picked it up."

"And the casing?"

Constable Braxton nodded his head. "Newman found it in one of the rose bushes."

Outdoor crime scenes were more difficult to assess than indoor ones, as it was impossible to dust for fingerprints, particularly when there was nothing about but lawn and foliage thinning out to prepare for winter.

Hoping for a clue, Ginger scoured the immediate area, around the body, and the distance from it to the house. Perhaps something had been dropped by the killer? But nothing as convenient as that presented itself.

The police photographer, Sergeant Scott, wearing his navy-blue buttoned-down police uniform and rounded helmet, was escorted in by Inspector Sanders. "Nasty, that," he said on seeing the body. He went to work immediately with his Brownie box camera.

"Take a few of the back of the house," Basil said, "particularly the doors."

"Yes, sir," Sergeant Scott said. He held the camera at waist-level, viewed the image through the glass on the top of the apparatus, and snapped. Thankfully, they still had late-afternoon light, and he didn't require a flash pan.

The pathologist arrived while they watched

Sergeant Scott work, much to the police photographer's relief, Ginger mused.

"Dr. Gupta!" Ginger said loudly. "It's been donkey's years."

Basil helped Ginger to her feet, and they approached the young pathologist. Dr. Manu Gupta was an attractive Indian man with creamy, dark skin and brilliant eyes, the colour of brass.

Ginger had once thought a romance might occur between the handsome man and her good friend Haley Higgins while Haley was a student at the London School of Medicine for Women, and Dr. Gupta worked in the school's mortuary. Alas, Dr. Gupta married a lady from his homeland of India, and Haley had returned to Boston to become a doctor of pathology herself.

"Mrs. Reed," Dr. Gupta returned. "How are you?"

"Very well, thank you. And Mrs. Gupta?"

"Little Deepak keeps her busy," Dr. Gupta said. "But he's a delight, nonetheless."

"Congratulations," Ginger said. "The Chief Inspector and I will endure sleepless nights ourselves, soon, as well." Though she and Basil would have a nanny to assist, it wasn't a point that needed stressing.

Dr. Gupta's eyes moved to Ginger's midsection for a split second. "My hearty congratulations to you both."

"Thank you."

"Now, I presume I've been called to examine a body?"

"This way, Doctor," Basil said.

Ginger stepped in behind as Basil led Dr. Gupta to the corpse of Mr. Beaulieu, lying just out of sight.

Dr. Gupta set his medical bag on the lawn and made his preliminary check for signs of life—placing two fingers at the neck and then the wrist—though it was obvious the man was deceased. After a quick examination of the body's positioning and a sniff for funny smells, he cut through Mr. Beaulieu's shirt to reveal discolouration of the skin.

"Gunpowder has burned his skin, indicating a shot at close range. I'll know more after the post-mortem," Dr. Gupta said. "Are you ready for the body to be removed?"

"I believe we have everything we need for now," Basil said.

"Very well," Dr. Gupta returned. "I'll bid you good afternoon."

When the pathologist left, Basil took Ginger's hands. "I have to stay to question those in Sanders' care. Should I ring a taxicab for you? Or I can get Braxton to give you a lift?"

"No, no," Ginger said. "I'd like to be part of the interviews."

"Are you sure? I'm quite capable."

"I know. And if it weren't Felicia's wedding, I would take you up on your offer, but I'd really like to hear what everyone has to say."

"Very well, Mrs. Reed," Basil said, linking his arm with hers. "Let's find Sanders."

The sitting room of Witt House was larger than the one at Hartigan House, though Ginger thought it could use a similar redecoration effort. The residence was rather stuck in the Edwardian age and hadn't, for many years since the death of Charles' mother, benefited from a feminine touch, and Ginger was certain Felicia wouldn't waste any time seeing to modernising it now that she was the lady of the house.

The walls were papered with a dramatic red and white floral design, and every inch covered in a framed painting of varying subjects from the seashore to family portraits and those of the royal line. Ornate wooden furniture upholstered in velvet and protected with crocheted antimacassars—a reminder of a time when Charles' mother was still alive—was positioned around a coffee table and facing a lit fireplace. Ceramic and porcelain figurines from India, Asia, and Africa, covered the mantel and the sideboard in the room, and Ginger imagined that the maids were kept busy with dusting.

There were more than enough seats for the few stragglers, those who hadn't yet left the party when the gun had gone off, who also were absent from the ballroom.

Harry Webster, his legs crossed at the knee, smoked a cigarette, and if one could go by the small mountain of butts in the ashtray standing at his elbow, he'd been smoking non-stop since being deposited there.

Pierre Dubois sat in his wheelchair, his fingers tapping nervously on the narrow wooden arms. His chin rested on his chest, and his eyes were closed, and Ginger felt pity for the man, who clearly was ready to take to his bed. A fit man would be exhausted by this excitement, as they all were, but the infirm had it particularly hard.

Miss Ward sobbed quietly in one of the winged chairs, her head bracing against one side. Whatever glamour and sophistication she'd started the late afternoon with had melted away with her tears, fatigue, and, quite likely, a hangover.

Mr. Hughes stoked the fire then took a nearby chair. He picked up a pipe sitting on a small side table and sucked on it as he held a match over the bowl.

Inspector Sanders greeted Ginger and Basil. "Oh, Chief Inspector, you folks have finished with the body, then?"

At this, Miss Ward's sobs wrenched into a higher gear. Mr. Webster reached over with a handkerchief which Miss Ward accepted.

"For now," Basil said. "I gather you've collected everyone's details?"

Inspector Sanders poked a small notebook with a stubby finger. "Righto, sir. Names and addresses. The lady lives at a boarding house. Mr. Hughes is a guest, having been here for just over a week. Mr. Webster is a Londoner but is staying here as well to assist Mr. Dubois. There is also an abundance of staff."

"Very good, Inspector," Basil said. "Is there a room where we could interview each one indi-vidually?"

Inspector Sanders pointed to the far side of the

room. "There's an adjoining area just beyond the archway. They call it a morning room."

"Good. While Mrs. Reed and I interview the witnesses, perhaps you could start with the staff." Basil said. "I understand they've been rounded up and are waiting in the kitchen?"

"Indeed, they are, sir." Inspector Sanders had his notepad and pencil in beefy hands. "I'll get right to it."

Ginger spoke softly to Basil. "Perhaps we should start with Miss Ward. It seems cruel to keep her longer than necessary."

"I concur." He waved to Constable Braxton, who'd just stepped into the sitting room. "Braxton?"

"Sir?"

"Where's Newman?"

"He left with the body, sir."

"I see. Mrs. Reed and I will be in the morning room. Please ask Miss Ward to join us."

"Yes, sir."

Once in the attached vestibule, a smaller, slightly less cluttered version of the sitting room, Ginger and Basil each took a chair.

"You're certain you're all right?" Basil asked. "I hate to say it, but you look dreadfully tired."

"I am, but nervous energy is keeping me going,"

Ginger said. "I don't think I could nap right now, even if I tried."

Constable Braxton returned with Miss Ward, who crumpled into the empty chair. "I can't believe it!" The skin around her eyes was blackened from running mascara. "Mrs. Reed, he was going to propose tonight! At least I thought so. I was so sure. And now? Why would anyone do this?"

Ginger patted the distraught lady on the knee. "I don't know, Miss Ward, but the police will do their best to find out."

Miss Ward cast a leery glance at Basil and Constable Braxton, who stood off to the side. She sniffed into her handkerchief. "You'll forgive me if I don't exactly trust the police."

"Why is that?" Ginger asked.

"No reason. Only, they've not been so good to me in the past."

"That sounds like a reason," Ginger said carefully. "What is it you do?"

"What do you mean?"

Basil interjected. "Do you have a profession?"

"I'm an actress. Though I don't see what that has to do with poor Jean-Claude."

"How did you get to know Mr. Beaulieu?" Basil asked.

"As I already told Mrs. Reed, we met in Paris, after one of my performances."

"Did you travel with Mr. Beaulieu from France?" Ginger asked. "Are you living there?"

"No, not any longer. I'm staying in London for now, at a boarding house. I'm about to start a new play."

"But you must've seen Mr. Beaulieu regularly?" Basil asked. "Did he travel to London often?"

"Not as often as I'd have liked," Miss Ward said. "But he was very busy with his job in Paris."

Basil tapped his pencil on his notepad. "Which was?"

"Oh, I don't know. Some business thing or other. He said he didn't want to bore me with it."

"What made you think he intended to propose tonight?" Ginger asked gently.

"He invited me to this wedding, didn't he? He didn't have to do that, and he was being so romantic before."

Hardly a sign that a man was intent on proposing, but Ginger hadn't been privy to the nuances of their relationship.

"Where were you when the gun went off, Miss Ward?" Basil asked.

"Actually, I was looking for Jean-Claude. We

were getting ready to leave. He helped me slip into my coat—" She motioned to the fur draped over one arm. "I fastened the buttons, and when I turned to thank him, he was gone."

"Was anyone else fetching their coats at the same time as you?" Ginger asked.

"No. It was just the two of us." Miss Ward released a heavy sigh. "I'm terribly upset. Can I go home now?"

Basil nodded. "Constable Braxton will ring for a taxicab. Please stay in London, Miss Ward. In case we have further questions."

With heavy shoulders, Miss Ward left the vestibule. Basil asked Constable Braxton to return with Mr. Dubois, which made Ginger shiver slightly with nerves. Would the man keep her secret? Ginger had done her part to keep her vow to the Crown and the Official Secrets Act, but she couldn't control the tongues of other people who knew. In a way, she'd be relieved if he blurted the truth to Basil. Ginger would love nothing more than to finally have that invisible barrier that occasionally slipped between them, finally and permanently removed.

CHAPTER EIGHT

*P*ierre Dubois' eyes latched on to Ginger as Constable Braxton rolled him into the vestibule. Ginger doubted the Frenchman enjoyed being moved about like a piece of luggage, at least his look of dismay would suggest such a thing. But it was a long way from the far end of the sitting room to where Ginger and Basil waited, and those rolling chairs could be rickety and hard to manoeuvre manually, especially moving from carpet to wooden floors and back.

"I 'ope zis will not take much longer," Mr. Dubois said, his accent growing stronger with his fatigue. He made a show of shifting uncomfortably in his chair. "My legs need to be stretched out. It ees not good for me to be in zis chair for so long. I 'ave pushed myself to come as eet is."

"We'll move along as quickly as we can," Basil said. "Is it safe for me to assume that you and Mr. Beaulieu were friends?"

"Oui." Mr. Dubois ran a hand through his hair, dishevelling it further. "We fought together in zee war. Along wiz Webster and Davenport-Witt. Men become like brothers on zee battlefield." He lowered his chin and stared at Basil. "Did you serve, Chief Inspector?"

Basil didn't flinch. "I did."

Ginger cast her husband a fleeting glance. Basil had served but was wounded in the first battle he'd fought in, losing his spleen. Invalided out of the armed services, he was sent back to London, where he'd started with the Met, serving his country in that regard. Although the son of an Honourable, when the war ended, and men of his social standing looked down their noses at police work, he continued.

"Zen you know what I mean. Davenport-Witt, naturally, invited us to 'is wedding—" He grinned crookedly in Ginger's direction, which had the disconcerting effect of creating a bend in his scar tissue. "Believe me, 'e could 'ave tied zee knot a dozen times in zee last ten years—and anyway, zat ees why I am 'ere."

"Are you saying that you and the deceased fought alongside British troops?" Basil asked.

"Sometimes zee British and zee French and indeed, zee American armies fought togezer as one. You seem to 'ave escaped unscathed."

Ginger glared at her husband's accuser. Had he somehow discovered that Basil had been invalided out of the war? Mr. Dubois wouldn't have been part of a spy network if he wasn't good at putting his nose where it didn't belong.

Mr. Dubois was unfazed by Ginger's show of displeasure. He tilted his head, and with a twinkle in his eye said, "'Ave we met before, Mrs. Reed?"

Ginger's heart beat double time. Was this it? Was the man about to expose her secret, once and for all?

Before she could respond, he snapped his fingers. "It 'as come back to me. You worked in France during zee war, no? Did you not frequent ze Bar du bonheur wiz your friends?"

Ginger let out a controlled breath. "I did, in fact. Your memory is phenomenal."

"Your beautiful red 'air ees 'ard to forget, madame."

Basil cleared his throat. "Mr. Dubois, did Mr. Beaulieu have any enemies?"

Mr. Dubois lifted a shoulder. "*C'est possible.* A foe could be anyone. It ees 'ard to tell a friend from an enemy zese days."

Ginger asked, "Can you think of a reason someone would want to harm him?"

With a pointed finger, Mr. Dubois drew circles near his temple. "Sanity ees an illusion. Zee war messes wiz zee mind."

"How did you come to London?" Basil asked. "You didn't travel alone, did you?"

"Crossed zee Channel from Calais to Dover. And no, as much as I would 'ave liked to, I did not travel alone. I journeyed wiz Webster."

"He was in France?" Ginger asked. "I thought he lived in London."

"'e 'as a 'ome in bose places." Mr. Dubois smirked. "Turns out one can make money when one 'as two working legs."

"Where were you when the gun went off, Mr. Dubois?" Basil asked.

Mr. Dubois huffed. "I will say, not in zee back garden." He tapped the wheels of his chair. "You might 'ave noticed a step down from zee French windows. I could not proceed with zis machine."

"Are you enjoying your stay in the guest house?" Ginger asked.

Mr. Dubois lifted his chin and smiled. "*Oui.* But I depend on *mon ami*, Webster, to get from 'ere to zere. Alas, zis fine 'ouse wasn't built wiz my chair in mind." He stared back at Basil. "To answer your question, Chief Inspector, I was in zee 'ouse when zee gunshot went off. At zee French windows, in zee study."

"Did you see who Mr. Beaulieu was with?" Ginger asked.

"If I 'ad, I would 'ave said so already. Sadly, I did not see zee keeller. Zee fountain and zee bushes were in my way. I am afraid zat I cannot 'elp you."

GINGER FELT she had the stamina for one more interview. "Perhaps we can finish with Mr. Webster tonight and delay our conversation with Mr. Hughes until tomorrow?"

Basil nodded. "I believe he'll be pleased with that arrangement, as well."

Harry Webster sauntered in, one fist buried in his trouser pockets. Casually, he lowered himself into an empty chair and slouched, with his long legs extended.

"Can we speed this up? My drinks have caught up with me; I have to go to the loo. And Dubois is waiting for me to push him to his room. This blasted affair has us both knackered and ready for a lie down."

"We'll go as quickly as we can," Basil said, frowning at the man's purposeful uncouthness. "We've already learned that you served in the war, at times, alongside Jean-Claude Beaulieu—"

"Who told you that?"

Basil stilled. "Are you saying it's not true?"

Mr. Webster's brow crumpled over his flattened nose as he shot a quick look at Ginger. "No, of course, it's true. We all served alongside someone we know, now and then."

"Mr. Dubois says you recently came with him from Paris, to attend this wedding," Ginger said. "Would you call France your home now? Or London?"

"I don't see what business it is of yours or the Yard's, but I suppose you can say London and Paris are both my homes. I have a modest house in Chelsea and a flat in Paris. I find I can relax there, you know? The French have an *appétit de vivre*, a flair for life, that I admire. When I'm there, I look in on Dubois."

"What happened to Mr. Dubois?" Basil asked. "In the war? Was he shot on the front line?"

Mr. Webster moved his lips as he placed a long finger on his chin. "He doesn't really like to talk about it. He was left for dead and spent some time as a prisoner. But, like I said, he refuses to talk about it. A dark time, you know. We all want to forget."

Again, a sideways glance in Ginger's direction. She kept her expression blank, hoping her eyes didn't reveal that she had caught the lie. Her recollection wasn't crystal clear, but she knew about a group of spies who were ordered to intercept and bomb a German train, and since these men were part of that network, they were either involved in that mission or knew those who were.

Instead, she asked, "Where were you tonight, when Mr. Beaulieu was shot?"

Mr. Webster removed a silver cigarette case, opened it, and revealed a lone cigarette. "I was smoking on the terrace. I'd taken Dubois down to the sitting room—he finds noise and activity tiring—and bored with my chit-chat, he shooed me away. I went back upstairs to the terrace. I didn't stand near the balustrade and didn't see what was happening below in the garden."

"Did anyone see you?" Basil asked.

After lighting the last cigarette with a silver lighter, he blew the smoke out of the side of his mouth. "I have no idea. I wasn't paying attention. A few couples had stepped out for fresh air, but they were focused on their companions. They'd come in from the reception room and I from the landing at the top of the steps, so I was concealed behind a potted plant."

A convenient alibi. "How well do you know Miss Ward?" she asked. A swift change in subject often set one on one's heels.

"Not well at all, Mrs. Reed," he said without missing a beat. "I only met her tonight."

CHAPTER NINE

The memory came to her in the early morning hours, but Ginger couldn't follow through on her thoughts until Basil had dressed and gone down for breakfast.

"I'll be down shortly," Ginger had said, reassuring him. When she was certain he'd gone down the staircase, she opened the drawer of her bedside table, reached to the back, and uncovered her old journal. The days of the war reminded her dearly of her loss of Daniel, and since marrying Basil, she had found it best to put it behind her, a part of her past life. Not dead, but figuratively buried.

As she read the entry, much of it in a code she'd devised for her own use, the memory flooded back.

January 15, 1917

The Plan

The meeting in Maubeuge, at an old farmhouse outside a French village near the front, took place in the early evening. The location, although behind enemy lines, was discreet and often used for covert discussions. A fresh, thick blanket of snow had fallen throughout the day, and the other operatives had problems negotiating the roads out to the farm. Because of this, the meeting was delayed until 10 p.m. Captain Smithwick and I travelled together, driving a rundown Fiat; we nearly went off the road twice.

Once gathered, Captain Smithwick and the others leaned over a large map spread out on a wooden table. He ran his fingers along a railway line starting in the German town of Aachen and running all the way west to Mons.

In French, he began, "According to our intelligence, the railway line from Mons to Liège is one of the main supply routes to this area of the front."

Two of our colleagues, men, stood around the table and stared at the point Captain Smithwick pointed to. Light from the dancing flames in the fireplace flickered on their faces.

"Operatives here and here have reported seeing more activity with troop movements." Captain Smithwick tapped his fingers on two small villages along the route. "An attack just west of Mons would be the most effective."

Claude, a tall Frenchman in his late twenties, wore a black shirt and wool cap. Leaning forward, he tapped on the map. "Here, just in the place where the forest is the thickest."

In his early twenties, the other Frenchman, who had introduced himself as "Pantin", scratched his bearded chin. "The gradient is steep, and the corner is sharp," he said. "The train might travel faster down that hill. Perhaps we can cause a few carriages to topple when they leave the track."

"Have the explosives arrived yet?" Captain Smithwick asked

"Yes, we got them yesterday," Claude answered. "Our men are ready to go with them."

"Well, if we can get enough operatives here and here," Captain Smithwick tapped again on the map, "we should be able to not only do some real damage to the railway line but also inflict some pain on the Boche."

"And fade into the night before they know what hit them," Pantin said with a chuckle.

"Isn't there a German garrison near there?" I asked. All three men watched me as I drew closer to the map. "There, at Jemappes."

"Yes, but that should not be of any concern," Captain Smithwick replied. "The raid will be carried out in the middle of the night, under cover of darkness. If the team is fast enough—"

I couldn't shake my concern. "Do we have information on when the garrison sends out their patrols?"

"So far, we have seen no patrols in the specific area," Captain Smithwick said, with a note of irritation in his voice. "At least, not of any significance. Isn't that right, Claude?"

The Frenchman took a deep breath before answering, "No. We have seen no patrols from the garrison."

"How long have you been watching them?" I asked. I looked at Claude but felt Captain Smithwick glaring at me.

Claude answered, "For about three days, mademoiselle."

I blew air out of my cheeks and stepped back from the map. "Usually, the Germans are pretty predictable, but still, that's only about two kilometres from—"

"I think it's pretty safe to say the area will be clear at that time."

Even though I was there to contribute to the planning and offer my ideas, the captain brushed me off.

It wasn't until we were halfway back to the village that Captain Smithwick finally spoke up in the car, voicing his trepidation. "There are no ideal circumstances. War is always a gamble." He tapped the steering wheel with his thumbs, his eyes steady on the road, "Everyone knows that."

He was the captain, the leader of my small network, and others that I wasn't privy to, so I had to trust his judgement. Still, I thought they could wait a little longer until more intelligence could be gathered to carry out the attack.

Ginger stared into the distance, suddenly back in that farmhouse, then in that rickety old car. A week after that meeting, news had spread quickly through the networks. The mission had failed. One man who survived the raid reported that they must have been spotted placing the explosives, perhaps by a German patrol from Jemappes, just as Ginger had feared.

It explained why, just as they were about to set off the explosives—the train barrelling down the track—they were set upon by a company of about twenty soldiers and were quickly overwhelmed.

A day later, a team of operatives finally went back to retrieve the dead. Ten French and English operatives were found lying on the snowy forest floor, with one missing and presumed dead. All had been shot multiple times.

Why this event was burned into Ginger's memory, she didn't know. She hurried as much as one could in her condition and hastened downstairs to meet Basil for breakfast, making a short stop at her study to deposit the journal in her desk drawer to read later.

CHAPTER TEN

As they had arranged, Basil and Ginger returned to Witt House in Belgravia. Having rung ahead, they were expected, and Charles' butler, Burton, showed them to the ground-floor sitting room, where Maximillian Hughes, the person they had requested to see, was drinking tea.

He stood as Basil and Ginger entered. "Good morning, Chief Inspector and Mrs. Reed!"

"Good morning," Basil and Ginger returned.

"Would you like to join me for a cup of tea?"

"We've just come from breakfast," Basil said, eager to begin. "If you don't mind, we'd like to get right to it."

"Oh yes," Hughes said amiably "How do you want to go about that?"

Basil thought he looked no worse for wear after a late night and more than a few drinks. "Just a few questions before we look around a bit more, if that's all right with you," he said.

Basil held Ginger's hand as she lowered herself into an empty chair, keeping her handbag on her lap. The ruse wouldn't last much longer, and Basil wondered if it had already stopped working some time ago. At least Hughes was gracious enough not to stare.

"Perhaps you can start by telling us how you know Charles," Basil started. "As it appears, he has given you the run of the house."

Hughes grinned. "We were both at Oxford when we were conscripted. We weren't yet close friends, but as fate would have it, we were thrown together on the battlefield." He smiled as he tapped his heart. "And now we're brothers."

"Charles also invited friends he'd met in France," Ginger said. "Were you friends with them as well? Mr. Dubois and the deceased, Mr. Beaulieu?"

Hughes sipped his tea slowly, then answered. "We'd met before, but I wouldn't call them friends."

"What about Mr. Webster?" Basil asked.

"We met up on occasion after the war. But again, I wouldn't say we were mates."

Ginger tucked a flyaway strand of red hair behind her ear. "Does the Belgian town of Jemappes mean anything to you, Mr. Hughes?"

"Er, no, not specifically. But our regiment went through many small towns. Why do you ask?"

Basil narrowed his gaze at Ginger, wondering the same thing.

"Oh, no reason," Ginger said, waving her gloved hand. "I just thought I heard someone mention it."

His wife was up to something, but that didn't surprise Basil. He'd long ago stopped trying to understand how her mind worked, embracing the mystery as part of the parcel of things he loved and admired about her. Still, he wished she'd confide in him more willingly. He'd been married to her long enough to figure out that she wasn't exactly an open book. He had no secrets and held nothing from her. He was quite sure she couldn't say the same. It always came back to the Great War.

"Where were you at the moment the pistol shot went off?" Basil asked.

"In the guest bedroom on the third floor. I'd developed a bleedin' headache and needed a quick lie down."

"Did anyone see you go up there?" Ginger asked. "A maid, perhaps?"

Hughes paused, then answered. "I can't say anyone did." He unfolded his legs and drew himself up. "Is there anything else I can do for you? I have a busy day ahead, and I shan't intrude on my friend's hospitality for much longer. I'm due back in Cardiff soon."

"Thank you for hanging back so we could speak, Mr. Hughes," Basil said. "You'll be remaining in Britain, should we have to speak further?"

Hughes blinked back a flash of annoyance. "Of course. Anything I can do to help, Chief Inspector."

Basil offered his arm to Ginger, who accepted the help to get to her feet. He worried she was doing too much and had even made a stop at Dr. Longden's surgery to ask him if his wife was overexerting herself. The doctor had reassured him that so long as she wasn't doing anything she wasn't already conditioned to do, she would be fine.

It was a comfort, but Basil still couldn't help feeling concerned from time to time.

"When we've finished here," he said, "perhaps we should return to Hartigan House for a rest."

Ginger patted his arm. "But we planned to stop at the mortuary after this."

"Righto. Then after that." Before Ginger could

protest, he added, "After last night, I could use putting my feet up."

They stepped into the ballroom where several maids were busy cleaning up.

"Inspector Sanders interviewed them all last night?" Ginger asked.

"Indeed," Basil said. He removed a folded piece of paper from his coat pocket. "I have a copy of his notes here."

"Anything of interest?"

Basil lifted a shoulder as he worked his lips. "The wedding reception was ending. Most of the staff were in cleaning-up mode, either in the ballroom or on the ground floor. Only one maid, Daphne Cook, claimed to be on the staircase at the time but couldn't recall seeing anything of import."

Ginger eyed the maid in the room. "Daphne?"

Basil grinned. It was a shot in the dark to see if the maid in question was present. They were rewarded when a young, pleasant-looking woman spun on her heel, and on seeing Ginger, curtsied. "Madam?"

"I don't mean to take you from your duties, but would you mind if we have a word?"

"Certainly, madam." The maid's eyes flickered with a touch of fear as she glanced at Basil.

He understood how certain classes viewed law-enforcers with suspicion. Hoping to disarm her, he softened his look.

"Please, don't be alarmed," he said. "We simply want to ask you a few questions about yesterday's tragedy. I understand that you were on the stairs at the time the pistol shot was heard."

"Yes, sir. I'd gone up to the third floor to, er, Mr. Hughes had requested a headache powder ..." She looked away, her cheeks blossoming with red patches. Basil wondered what the maid had to be embarrassed about. Perhaps she'd developed a crush on Charles' Welsh guest.

"Where were you precisely," Basil asked.

The maid's gaze shot to the floor. "On my way back to the ballroom, sir."

"Did anyone see you?" Ginger asked.

"No, madam."

"Thank you, Daphne," Basil said. He handed her his official calling card. "You'll seek me out if you hear anything that may help find the person who committed this awful crime?"

"Yes, sir." Daphne curtsied again, then returned to her dusting, which she did with renewed energy.

Basil rubbed his chin. "Did you find that odd?"

"I did," Ginger agreed. "I wonder why Mr.

Hughes failed to mention the maid. She would've provided him with a decent alibi."

"It must've slipped his mind," Basil said. "Men of his stature are so used to ignoring the staff that they become invisible, even if they are in direct sight."

GINGER WOULDN'T HAVE BEEN SURPRISED if Daphne, who'd now slipped out of the ballroom, hadn't found a fantasy involving Mr. Hughes appealing. The gentleman had an endearing quality. However, the maid wasn't a serious suspect, and according to Inspector Sanders' report, not only were none of the staff connected with Mr. Beaulieu, but also, they'd never laid eyes on him before the wedding reception.

She took a moment to take in the ballroom with its high ceilings, long windows draped in gold, and impressive electric chandelier, and then closed her eyes to recall the events of the night before. "We'll have to rely on our imaginations," she said.

Basil took her hand and gently led her to the middle of the floor. "We're standing in the exact spot we were when the shot rang out. Dancing, together."

"I had my head on your shoulder," Ginger said, "and I remember feeling exhausted but entirely content. The band played the last note, and I looked for Felicia, then remembered that she and Charles had left."

Ginger paused, her thinly plucked eyebrows arched.

"Yes?" Basil prompted.

"I was focused on you." She smiled at Basil, and he smiled in return.

"It was a lovely dance," he said. "But that's not what's bothering you."

"No, it's just—let's have a look at the terrace."

"And the cloakroom in the entrance hall," Basil said.

Ginger linked her arm in Basil's. "Yes, of course." It would be prudent to mark the areas where all their suspects had claimed to be.

They stepped into the corridor, took the stairs down to the ground floor, and then hurried along the corridor until they reached the cloakroom.

Besides Ginger's coat, which had been taken earlier by Burton, Charles' white-haired butler, hung a lady's fur-trimmed wool coat. "Someone forgot this gorgeous coat," Ginger said.

"I'm sure once whoever it was has slept it off, she'll be ringing the house."

Ginger removed it from the hanger. "I'll try it on and pretend to be Miss Ward."

"And I'll try to leave without you noticing."

Basil helped Ginger into the coat. The silk lining felt luxurious, and as if she were attempting the task in a state of intoxication, she took her time with the large buttons. When she finished with the fourth button, she spun around, and Basil was nowhere in sight.

"Her claim is credible," she said loudly as she unfastened the buttons.

Basil reappeared in the corridor, took the coat off Ginger's shoulders, and hung it back on the rod in the coat room.

"The question then is why did Mr. Beaulieu leave Miss Ward behind?"

"Perhaps he'd been called away," Basil responded, "quietly, so that Miss Ward didn't hear."

"Can we be sure this is the way the killer went out into the garden?" Ginger asked. They had returned to the study. She stood at the French door and peered through the window.

"According to Braxton, the study door wasn't properly closed," Basil said. "The door leading out from the vestibule was closed but not locked."

"The study door could've been innocently left

unlatched and with the wind catching it," Ginger said. "It doesn't mean the killer used it."

"Indeed," Basil agreed. "The killer accessed the garden from either the study or the vestibule off the sitting room. But I'm leaning towards the study."

"I am too," Ginger said. "The chance of being seen by someone resting in the sitting room, such as Mr. Dubois, would've been too great."

Basil opened the door and paused at the step that led to the back garden.

"Mr. Dubois claims to have rolled himself to this point before the shot," Ginger said. "Having heard a commotion and loud talking."

They stepped into the garden, walking to the spot where Mr. Beaulieu's body had been found.

"Where would he have been standing before he fell to the ground?" Ginger asked.

The ground had been marked where the body had lain. Basil took one step away from where the feet had been.

"About here, I imagine."

"Dr. Gupta said the shot was from close range, which I take to be at most six feet." Ginger took a position six feet back from Basil. "The killer must've fired a shot from here."

"That seems correct."

Ginger waved a hand, motioning for Basil to join her. "Come and take my place."

Basil did as she asked.

"Wait here. I want to check something." Ginger left Basil on his mark and returned to the doorway where Pierre Dubois claimed to have been. She frowned.

"What is it?" Basil called out.

"There really isn't anything obscuring the sight line." Ginger carefully crouched to where Mr. Dubois would've been watching from a seated position. "He said the fountain and the bushes were in the way, but the fight had to have taken place between the fountain and the guest house. It's odd that he didn't see who was with Mr. Beaulieu. I can see the area from here."

Basil joined her at the step. "Why would he lie?"

"Perhaps he's protecting someone?"

"Miss Ward?" Basil asked. "Or Mr. Webster?"

Or Charles, but Ginger didn't speak that aloud. Charles could've had the means and opportunity and possibly even a motive, but she couldn't believe that he would choose his own wedding night to carry out such a nefarious deed. The idea was too preposterous.

"Or Mr. Hughes?" she said. "They are all

connected to Mr. Beaulieu. We just need to figure out how. It's possible one of them held a grudge."

Basil huffed. "We are dreadfully shy of motives at the moment."

Ginger agreed.

They enquired of a maid as to how to find where Mr. Hughes had spent the night—which was three floors up—and determined it was far away from the crime scene, but it only removed suspicion of guilt if one could prove he was there.

Mr. Webster had claimed to be smoking on the terrace but couldn't provide a witness. He could've slipped down one floor, though it was hard to imagine that someone wouldn't have seen him.

Having gone over the events of the evening, Basil suggested they leave for the mortuary. Ginger agreed. The butler was waiting for them with her coat.

"Please thank Mr. Hughes for his time and cooperation," Basil said.

"I will, sir," came the polite reply.

Basil took Ginger's arm. "Are you ready for the mortuary?"

CHAPTER ELEVEN

Ginger had been invited to the University College Hospital mortuary on Westmoreland Street more times than she could count. Despite the frequency, she still wrinkled her nose as she stepped lower into the basement where the scent of bleach grew stronger, and then once through the metal door, the smell of death.

Underneath a large lamp that did the work of dispelling the cellar grimness, the long, lean body of Jean-Claude Beaulieu lay on a white porcelain table in the poorly lit room. Refrigerated cabinets, a new advancement, were installed along the back wall, shrinking the room's size. One of them was now reserved for Mr. Beaulieu.

"Hello, Dr. Gupta," Ginger said.

Basil tipped his hat. "Doctor."

Dr. Gupta wore a white smock and held a clipboard in his hand.

"I hope all is well at home," Ginger said. "How is Mrs. Gupta and the baby?"

"They are well. My mother-in-law arrives from India next weekend, so I'm hoping we all get more sleep then."

Ginger smiled knowingly. "Children are a blessing, even when they rob us of sleep." She laughed. "At least that's what I'm counting on."

Basil brought the meeting to the point. "What have we got, Dr. Gupta? Anything new to report?"

Dr. Gupta referred to his clipboard before putting it aside. "As we assumed at the scene, the deceased died immediately from a gunshot wound to the heart. But—" He stepped up to the body, pulled the sheet from the corpse's head and down to its waist, and revealed the Y-incision, now stitched with thick stitching.

"These contusions on the shoulder area are fresh, and the autopsy revealed that the shoulder had been dislocated."

"From his fall?" Ginger asked. "After he was shot?"

"I'd assumed that at first as well," Dr. Gupta said,

"but that would mean that Mr. Beaulieu had a history of shoulder dislocation. A normal fall wouldn't have resulted in a dislocation otherwise. But there's no evidence that he'd ever suffered a dislocation before. No scarring around the ligaments or markings on the bone."

"Are you saying that Mr. Beaulieu had his shoulder dislocated by someone before he was shot?" Basil asked.

Dr. Gupta nodded. "That is what the forensic evidence suggests."

"Are you certain he was standing when shot?" Ginger said. "Could someone have shot him by standing over him while he was down?"

"As I mentioned at the scene, gunpowder wounds suggest the pistol went off at close range, around six feet. Any closer and the heart would've shown more significant damage. To shoot him at the angle the bullet entered, the killer would have to be standing on top of him. The evidence for that simply is not there."

After saying goodbye to Dr. Gupta, Ginger and Basil left the hospital and stopped at a nearby café for a bite to eat. Ginger found she was hungry more often than usual, and Basil was always game for a meal. Despite settling for comfort over fashion when it came to her footwear—she missed her leather T-strap shoes and designer pumps, having settled for plain slipper-style shoes, the kind Ambrosia had taken to wearing—her ankles were swollen, and her feet ached.

She ordered tea and crumpets with butter and jam, and as they nibbled and sipped, they discussed the case.

"Whoever shot Mr. Beaulieu wrestled with him first," Ginger said. "Then when they broke away, Mr. Beaulieu thought the worst was over . . . then his wrestler shot him."

"You've obviously never dislocated a shoulder," Basil said.

"I have not," Ginger admitted.

"I have, as a youth. My horse became spooked and bucked me off. I landed on my shoulder and believe me, it was agonising."

"Thank goodness you didn't land on your head."

Basil grinned. "I love how you always see the bright side."

"Ha," Ginger returned. "So, you're saying that Mr. Beaulieu would've yelled or at least spent more time on the ground writhing before getting to his feet to be shot at point-blank range."

"The timeline doesn't seem to fit," Basil said.

"Unless it wasn't accidental from a wrestling match, but intentional. Someone who knew exactly what he was doing."

"Like a former soldier," Ginger said. "But why? If one were intent on killing a man and had a gun, why not just shoot and dispense with the theatrics?"

"Perhaps he sought to avenge and not merely to have his revenge."

Ginger wrinkled her nose. "The killer wanted Mr. Beaulieu to feel pain first. But we're back to the problem of not hearing him scream."

"The band was rather loud," Basil said. "I don't expect that anyone in the ballroom would've heard him yell, not from that far away."

"However, Mr. Dubois was in the doorway, and Mr. Webster and Miss Ward were in the corridor and the cloakroom." Ginger said. "Is it possible that more than one person was involved? Miss Ward could've easily lured Mr. Beaulieu out to the garden on the prospect of romance."

"Webster could've damaged the man's shoulder."

"And Miss Ward could've fired the shot."

"Unfortunately," Basil said, "we've yet to find the murder weapon."

Serendipity sometimes presents itself, and before the words were completely out of Basil's mouth,

Constable Braxton breezed into the café. He hurried over when he spotted Ginger and Basil at their table.

"Sir," he said, "Dr. Gupta said I might find you here."

"You've found us, Constable," Basil said. "I assume you have news."

"I do, sir. We've found a pistol that matches the bullet and the casing."

Basil placed coins on the table to take care of the bill. "That's great news," he said. "Has the lab dusted for prints?"

"Yes, sir." The constable's eyes flashed darkly as he glanced at Ginger.

"What is it, Constable?" Ginger asked.

"Madam, there weren't any fresh prints as the gunman must've worn gloves, but the serial number shows the service pistol had been registered to Lord Davenport-Witt. The weapon was discovered in a drawer in a filing cabinet in Lord Davenport-Witt's study."

CHAPTER TWELVE

The Ritz Hotel was a luxurious choice for a wedding night. Ginger was reluctant to interrupt Felicia and Charles, but this new development demanded it. Fortunately, the couple wasn't in a private or embarrassing situation—they were having a cosy luncheon at one of the tables in the restaurant. The concierge had been kind enough to direct Ginger and Basil to the newlyweds.

"Ginger!" Felicia said when she spotted them. Wearing a royal-blue crepe day frock with a matching tie-collar, inverted shoulder tucks, and a bold multi-coloured print on the bodice, Felicia blushed like a new bride under her blue and white cloche hat.

"Oh, how lovely! You're just in time for dessert!

We've ordered apricot tarts. We'll order for you as well." She squeezed Charles' hand. "Isn't this fabulous, Charles? Ginger and Basil have come to celebrate with us."

Ginger glanced Basil's way before taking the empty chair across from the couple.

"Please don't order on our account," Ginger said.

Felicia frowned. "Oh dear. Don't tell me you've come with bad news. I just can't bear it. Can't we have at least one day of joy?"

"I'm dreadfully sorry, darling," Ginger said. "But a man has died."

"Oh, I know," Felicia returned with a pout. "Charles told me the dreadful news. Forgive me for being a pill."

"You have a right to expect happiness when you get married," Ginger said. "I'm sorry things are turning out this way."

Felicia huffed in defeat. "Can't be helped."

"What have you discovered?" Charles asked. "Have you found the culprit?"

"Not yet," Basil said. "But we have found the murder weapon."

"Well, that's great news," Felicia said. "Who does it belong to? That person must be the killer."

Ginger swallowed. "It was found in your study, Charles."

"*What?*" Charles stiffened. "I don't keep any weapons in my study!"

Felicia blanched. "Someone placed it there," she said, "to frame Charles!"

"That's not all of it, I'm afraid," Basil said.

Charles groaned. "Don't tell me it's one of my guns."

Basil caught his eye. "Why would you say that?"

"Because if it weren't, you'd just tell us, instead of all this cloak and dagger."

"Very well," Basil said. "The serial number belongs to your registered service pistol."

"Charles!" Felicia cried. "How can this be?"

"I assure you, I don't know," he said. "My service pistol went missing before I could surrender it to the British government. Someone has got hold of it and intends to frame me."

"It's what we believe as well," Ginger said, though a nudge by Basil's knee informed her she shouldn't have spoken for him. "However," she continued, "we need to work out who would want to both kill Jean-Claude Beaulieu and frame you."

"Agreed," Charles said. "Who are your prime suspects?"

"I'm afraid they're all friends of yours," Basil said. "Guests you invited to the wedding."

"I presumed so," Charles said. "Webster and Dubois."

"Also, Miss Ward," Basil said. "And we can't rule out Mr. Hughes."

"Charles," Ginger started, "can you think of any reason why someone, particularly any of these people, would want to harm Mr. Beaulieu?"

Charles ran a hand through his hair, smoothing it to one side. "Honestly, I can't imagine Webster or Dubois doing such a thing. The war brought us together, closer than brothers. And Dubois depends on Webster. Where one goes, there goes the other."

"If you don't mind my saying," Basil said, "you don't seem particularly broken up by your friend's death."

"I suppose I've learned to compartmentalise, Basil." He took Felicia's hand. "I'm trying to save what happy memories are left for my bride."

"Mr. Dubois' wheelchair was prevented from going into the back garden because of a step," Basil said, "so we can rule him out for now. What can you tell us about Mr. Webster's relationship with Mr. Beaulieu, besides the fact that they were 'brothers'?"

"Well, Webster and Beaulieu are . . . were . . .

what you could call 'ladies' men', and in France and Belgium, they often had friendly, er . . ." he glanced sheepishly at Felicia and Ginger. ". . . competition. Which of them could entice the prettiest lady in the public house."

"Might one infer that Miss Ward was now involved in that competition?" Ginger said.

Charles held her gaze. "One might."

"I'm afraid I'm going to have to ask you to postpone your wedding journey for a couple of days," Basil said. "Just until we get to the bottom of things."

"No!" Felicia said. "I've got my heart set on sunning on the beach of a Greek island."

"We can extend our time, darling," Charles said. "But, as my duty as Jean-Claude's friend, I'm compelled to stay." He ran a finger along her jawline. "We'll eat caviar and drink champagne as we watch the sun set on the Thames. It'll be lovely, I promise."

Felicia relented with a weak smile.

Basil cleared his throat. "I hate to have to ask you this, Davenport-Witt. But where were you when the pistol shot went off?"

Charles blinked back, looking flustered. "Felicia and I had already left."

After a pause, Felicia said softly, "But we hadn't, darling. You ran back inside to fetch my handbag."

"Oh, deuced bad luck," Charles said, slapping his knee. "But I honestly didn't hear it for what it was. I thought a motorcar had backfired."

Ginger squinted back at the earl. She'd wanted to believe that to be the case, but immediately knew otherwise. Surely a man such as Charles Davenport-Witt, trained with the special services and experienced on the battlefields of France, would've discerned the difference as well.

Then again, perhaps time away from weapons of war, and the enthusiasm of newly married love had dulled his senses.

Ginger sincerely hoped so.

CHAPTER THIRTEEN

Ginger, feeling afternoon fatigue that had become usual for her, asked Basil to drop her off at Hartigan House. What she needed was a nice cup of tea and to put her feet up. Besides, she had work she could do from her desk in her study. Though Madame Roux did a marvellous job managing Feathers & Flair, Ginger couldn't entirely ignore her dress shop.

Upon Ginger's request, Lizzie immediately added coal to the study fireplace, and Pippins, the dear, brought the tea. Boss, recognising his mistress' voice—and no doubt the way her heels clicked along the black-and-white tiled floors and echoed along the high ceiling—followed her inside. He had a little bed by the hearth—there was one in every room—but came to Ginger first for approval and affection, his stubby tail wagging furiously.

"Oh, Bossy, you cute little thing!" Ginger kissed his black-and-white head and scratched his ears. The space on her lap he regularly occupied hadn't been available for some weeks, but his canine instincts seemed to sense her delicate condition, and he didn't act offended in the least. As if to underscore the sentiment, he licked her neck then trotted to his bed, where he curled into himself and closed his brown eyes.

The study had been her father's, and Ginger couldn't believe that he'd been gone for almost five years. She reclined in a new chair, the old one had been too large and worn out, and put her feet on a small stool. The study was the one room in the house that Ginger hadn't redecorated back in '23 and '24 after she'd returned from Boston and stayed on. The wood was dark, as was the wallpaper, and the shelves held many of her father's tomes on banking and business. A painting of him in his youth hung on the wall beside the fireplace. Ginger looked more like her mother, but there was something about her father she liked to claim belonged to her: his drive to succeed balanced out by a heart that saw the good in everyone.

As Ginger sipped her tea, her reverie turned to the present situation and poor Felicia, being held hostage at the Ritz when she'd wish to be away on her honeymoon to Greece. Ginger couldn't help but think of Daniel and how proud he'd be of his little sister, if not a little worried about her choice of groom.

Ginger would be far less worried had Daniel still been around to shoulder her concern. But alas, Daniel was no longer with them. It was worse for Felicia, Ginger had to remember, as she would never have another brother, but Ginger had found another love.

Thinking of Daniel brought her mind to the war, something she worked hard at forgetting, but this blasted case wouldn't be solved unless she allowed her mind to go back there; she was certain of it. All the suspects, along with the victim, were associated with that time, and—

Ginger sat upright.

Opening her desk drawer, she removed her journal. A particular entry was tickling her mind, and she flicked through the pages until she found it. Ah, yes. She remembered it well.

January 16, 1917.

The Fallout

As Captain Smithwick and I entered the old farmhouse once again, I was hit with the smells of stale cigarette smoke, horse manure, and oakwood burning in the old pot-bellied stove, which filled the room with the sounds of crackling as the damp wood struggled to burn. Claude, the tall Frenchman I'd met the last time we gathered there, sat at the wooden table, smoking a hand-rolled cigarette. His hand quivered as he lifted it to his mouth and inhaled. He ran a sleeve under his nose, and his watering eyes blinked rapidly as if he were trying to gather his wits.

Captain Smithwick presented a bottle of cheap whisky. The glasses we'd used last time were still in the sink, and I quickly rinsed out three of them, drying them with the hem of my skirt.

"We did not stand a chance," Claude said. He lifted the whisky to his lips and took a big gulp. "Those swine! They appeared out of nowhere."

"Do you think someone warned them?" Captain Smithwick asked. He hadn't shaved for a few days and his blues eyes, usually sharp and clear, were red and puffy from lack of sleep. "We think there could have been a double agent, a spy who went to Jemappes to warn the garrison."

I shot Captain Smithwick a look of surprise. I had heard no one present this as a theory.

"I do not know about that," Claude said. "I assumed a German patrol had seen us and had raced back for support without us knowing."

I recalled the concern I had voiced on the night the raid was planned, that the German outpost was too close. "It is only a short distance," I said, looking straight at the French operative. I kept my eyes from Captain Smithwick as I didn't want to appear to challenge my superior.

"Yes," Claude agreed.

"How many of them were there, do you think?" I asked.

"At least forty, maybe more, mademoiselle. We heard the sound of their vehicles first, then came the lights, and shouting in German. We scattered in all directions as those blasted Maxim MGs opened on us. Bodies everywhere. We were outnumbered!"

Since coming to France, I'd become an expert at swallowing whisky, and now seemed a good time to indulge. I let out a hot breath as the liquid burned down my throat.

"You are the only survivor of the skirmish that we know of," Captain Smithwick said as he refilled our three glasses. "Did you see anyone taken prisoner?

Claude swore. "They got Pantin."

His jaw clenched as he closed his eyes. Though he hadn't moved, his breath became quick and short. "I ran into the forest, hid, and then raced to a lookout on the small mountain beside the railway route. From there, I saw a group of German soldiers heading back on the road towards Jemappes. Pantin, holding his head in agony, was being dragged along the road."

He gulped his whisky, wiping his lips with the back of his hand. "A moment later, the train came down the tracks. The one we were supposed to blow up."

"Did you go back down to check for survivors?" Captain Smithwick asked.

"No, sir." Claude turned his attention back to his cigarette and took a long drag. "Two Boche were coming up the side of the mountain. They had tracked me through the snow. I ran down the other side of the mountain, and I didn't stop running for hours. At one point, I ran a few hundred metres down a shallow brook to break my trail. I'm glad they didn't have dogs with them." He chuckled, but it was humourless. "As they will tell you in the village, I collapsed inside the door of the church. The priest found me soon after."

Afterwards, once Claude had been dismissed, Captain Smithwick and I stood on the farmhouse's porch. The captain lit his pipe and leaned against the wooden panelling while I leaned on the hewn railing.

"He could be lying," he said as he waved out his match. "He could be the one who tipped off the Boche."

"I am not sure how," I said. "How could he have gone to . . ."

"I don't know," he snapped. "Perhaps he informed them with the help of someone else. Perhaps even before the operation had started."

I considered this for a moment. "I suppose so, but—"

"But what?"

"I think he's telling the truth, at least about that."

"I'm the one who taught you how to tell if a man is lying."

I countered, "And everything you taught me tells me this man is not lying. I don't think he knew about the German counter-attack."

There was a moment's silence between us.

Captain Smithwick sniffed in frustration, looked out into the night, and lifted the pipe to his mouth, holding it between his teeth. The embers burned red in the dark as he inhaled, giving his features a ghoulish look.

"Spider is missing."

"Spider?" It was the first time I'd heard this unusual handle.

"A British operative who joined the mission last minute. If he switched . . ." The captain shook his head. "All of our operations could be compromised."

"This Spider could be dead," I said. "Even without a body to prove it."

Captain Smithwick snorted. "It takes months to set up a network. People risk their lives just to allow for it. A bakery hires a certain helper, a mother suddenly encounters a long-lost sister, a city official brings on a new staff member. All under the watchful eye of the dratted Germans."

"I know," I said simply. I had helped set up such situations and was posing as someone else continually.

He looked at me, his expression grim. I wondered if the strain of leadership was taking its toll on him. It seemed he had doubted himself, a trait that could get people killed.

"I'll find this Spider and find out what he knows."

Captain Smithwick stared into the darkness. "Yes, Mademoiselle LaFleur. See to it."

CHAPTER FOURTEEN

*I*nstead of heading back to his office at the Yard after dropping Ginger off at Hartigan House, Basil steered his Austin toward Wilton Crescent, hoping to find Harry Webster and Pierre Dubois still in residence in the guest house. They weren't there, but the butler, fortunately, had overheard the name of the hotel bar where they had gone.

As luck would have it, Basil arrived in time to see Webster hoist Dubois out of his chair, scoop him by the waist, and drag him and his chair (in a far from graceful manner) up the steps and into the lounge. Dubois was then deposited back into the wheelchair, and both men took a moment to straighten their suits. With a swooping motion of one long arm,

Webster picked up both their hats which had fallen to the floor during the spectacle.

A moment of quiet descended in the lounge as other patrons stared, some watching discreetly and others rudely gawking. Webster pushed Dubois toward an empty table, knocking into one of the gawkers.

"Oh, terribly sorry," Webster said loudly when the man protested. "Please do pardon us."

Basil waited by the door until the two men were settled then, holding his hat in his hand, put on a large smile as he approached them.

"Mr. Webster and Mr. Dubois! Just the two gentlemen I was looking for."

Both men frowned, but then Webster forced a smile. "Quite fortuitous, I'd say. Would you like to join us?"

"I'd be delighted," Basil said, taking an empty chair. "Thank you."

Webster and Dubois each ordered a gin and tonic, and had Basil not been on the job, he would've loved to have joined them. He ordered soda water instead.

"Are you enjoying London, gentlemen?" Basil asked jovially.

"I razer 'ate zee city," Dubois said, his nose in the air. "Entirely barbaric compared to Paris."

"Yes, well, the English have this fascination with progress," Basil said. "I can see the appeal to a more relaxed existence."

"London's jolly well the best place on earth," Webster said. "Though, there's nothing quite like a beautiful French *fille*."

Basil laughed, hoping to put Webster and Dubois off guard. It helped when the drinks arrived, and the men each took long gulps.

Webster held his glass in the air. "To Davenport-Witt! The blighter's found his ball and chain!" Dubois chortled as he clinked glasses and added, "And poor Beaulieu, who no longer has to concern himself with that."

Basil scowled at their poor taste. "What do you mean, Mr. Dubois?"

Dubois' dark brows jumped. "About what?"

"That Mr. Beaulieu no longer has to concern himself with a ball and chain?"

"I was simply jesting," Dubois said stiffly.

"About whom?" Basil asked. "Miss Ward?"

Dubois snorted. "Yes, if you must force me to be so pointed."

Webster waved a hand as he casually crossed his

legs at the knees. "Beaulieu was never going to propose." He produced his cigarette case and lighter and lit up, blowing smoke into the already stuffy room.

Basil caught Webster's eyes. "Did Miss Ward know that?"

After a shrug, Webster answered, "Who's to say?"

"How well do you know Miss Ward?"

Webster kept a straight face, but Dubois' lips pulled up crookedly. "In zee way zee Bible defines 'ow to 'know' a woman."

Webster snapped. "Shut it, Dubois. Or you'll be pushing yourself out of this room."

Dubois' countenance darkened, and he returned to his drink.

"You gentlemen were pals with Lord Davenport-Witt during the war?" Basil said.

"Correct," Webster said. "We'd hardly get invited to his wedding otherwise." A waiter walked by, and Webster snapped his fingers. "Another, if you will."

"Yes, but you might've been friends by another means," Basil said. "However, it's come to my attention that you three, along with Mr. Beaulieu, had formed a strong bond during that time."

"What of it?" Webster said. "It's hardly original."

"No, except that now, one of you is dead."

"Please, keep reminding us," Dubois said. "I am not drunk enough yet."

"I do apologise for having to bring up the loss of your friend." Another thought occurred to Basil that caused him to pause before asking. "My wife was in France during the war. She worked as a telephone operator near Paris. Did you happen, by chance, to meet her there?"

Both Webster and Dubois stilled, only briefly, and a man not versed in studying people with a developed eye for detail might have missed it.

"No," Webster said with a grin. "I'd have remembered her, Chief Inspector. Your missus is, forgive me, a beauty."

Dubois joined in. " 'ow did you snap 'er up, anyway? No offence, but she could 'ave picked anyone."

Webster howled as if Dubois were a funny radio personality.

Basil smiled in return. "It was a long shot, I know."

Webster and Dubois were lying to his face. Ginger had recognised their names on the guest list and was concerned enough to request a police presence, and rightly so. If she knew them, they likely knew her. Yet, all parties denied it.

The question was, why?

What happened to this band of brothers in the war, and how, if at all, did it lead to one of them being murdered? And what did Ginger know about it?

Webster ordered another round of drinks, then knocked a long rope of ash into the ashtray in the middle of the table. "You know, Chief Inspector, Miss Ward—and I hate to speak ill of a lady behind her back—but she's the fragile type."

Dubois nodded. "Zose are zee most dangerous kind." He punched Webster in the arm. "Per'aps you should watch your back, *mon ami*."

CHAPTER FIFTEEN

With everything that had happened, Ginger hadn't got to the brunette who had interrupted the wedding ceremony. If death hadn't followed that outburst, it would be the event that everyone would remember and gossip about.

Who was the brunette?

Did she have anything to do with the murder? Or was it just an unpleasant coincidence?

Though coincidences certainly happened in life, as an investigator, Ginger had learned that it was prudent not to leave any stone unturned. She picked up the black telephone receiver, pleased to have got rid of the more cumbersome candlestick variety, and dialled the operator.

"Please connect me to Scotland Yard," she said. "It's not an emergency." After a few moments, a clerk answered. "Would you be so kind as to connect me to Chief Inspector Basil Reed?"

"I'm afraid the chief inspector's not in his office, madam."

"Oh, I see. This is Mrs. Reed. Is Constable Braxton available, or perhaps Constable Newman?"

"Constable Braxton is here, madam. Just a moment, please."

Ginger listened to the rattling that reached her through the line and then heard the familiar, youthful voice of Constable Braxton.

"Mrs. Reed, Constable Braxton here. How may I help you?"

"I'd like to locate the woman who interrupted Miss Gold's, er, rather, Lord and Lady Davenport-Witt's—" That handle would take some getting used to. "—wedding ceremony. You and Chief Inspector Reed walked her out of St. George's Church. Did you get her name and address?"

"I did, madam, as a matter of course. Give me a moment please, and I'll fetch the information for you."

A few minutes later, Ginger had her information. She looked at Boss who sat on his haunches in eager expectation. "Bossy, do you want to go for a motorcar ride?"

GINGER DROVE INTENTLY through the city, and Boss didn't seem the slightest bit unsettled, even when Ginger knocked a tyre into the kerb, though he lost his footing, slightly falling into the soft leather seat.

She read the numbers on the door of the building across the street. "This is the place, Bossy. Should we just march up and knock?"

Before Ginger could completely hook the leash to Boss' collar, the building's door opened, and the brunette stepped out. After turning a key in the lock and twisting the knob to ensure the door was locked, she walked along the pavement in the other direction.

"Come on, Boss," Ginger said quietly. Fortunately, it was a quiet street, and Ginger made it across uneventfully, holding one hand under her stomach for support. She hoped the brunette didn't plan to go far, and if she could go by the high heels and fancy red day frock, Ginger suspected she didn't.

She could've called to the woman—Constable Braxton had informed her that the lady's name was Miss Estelle Vasseur—but Ginger was curious where Miss Vasseur was headed and, more importantly, if she was planning to meet anyone.

Ginger had chosen a brown felt hat adorned with faux fruit, which sat at an angle on her head. It had a wider brim to shield her face, and on the one occasion when Miss Vasseur glanced over her shoulder, Ginger was quick to look down and fuss with a button on her coat so as not to catch her eye.

A café on the corner came into view, and Ginger was grateful when Miss Vasseur paused in front of it before opening the door and taking the single step up to get inside. Ginger scooped Boss into her arms and followed Miss Vasseur inside, taking a table down the row from the where Miss Vasseur sat, window-side.

She pushed Boss flat beside her. "Lie down." She pressed a finger to her lips to instruct him to be quiet. Many café owners didn't blink at the sight of a dog on-premises, but Ginger didn't want to take the chance of drawing attention to herself.

Aha, the lady intended to meet someone, as she ordered a pot of tea for two. Ginger's curiosity was piqued. She also ordered tea, keeping her voice low, and her face turned from Miss Vasseur's line of sight. Ginger didn't have reason to believe Miss Vasseur knew of her or cared if she did, but her companion might, and Ginger wanted to stay inconspicuous for as long as possible.

The tea was lovely, and Ginger enjoyed her cup, though it was her second of the afternoon, and she was in danger of bloating and floating away. She'd taken time to visit the bathroom at Hartigan House before she left, but these days found she was blazing a trail to the facilities, wherever they might be.

Miss Vasseur let out a long, sad sigh, and Ginger wondered if the lady was about to be stood up. Then the door opened, and in walked Harry Webster.

Interesting.

Mr. Webster looked a little wobbly on the feet, and Ginger thought he might already be in his cups, despite the early hour. He took Miss Vasseur's delicate hand in his. "Estelle. You are as beautiful as ever."

"Thank you."

Miss Vasseur wasn't exhibiting false humility. The French lady was the sight of feminine beauty with shiny dark hair cut in a short bob, the tips curled into circles that rested on rosy cheeks. Her eyes were brightened with blue eyeshadow that reached her thinly arched eyebrows. Her lips were tiny bows, thickly painted with red lipstick, and Ginger had no doubt she had a similar effect on all the men she met as she had on Mr. Webster.

And at one time, Charles.

"You are late," she said with a thick French accent.

"I got held up. That copper, Reed? Tracked me down for a chat."

Ginger sat up at the sound of Basil's name.

"The one who escorted me out of zee church?"

"Yes."

She smiled whimsically. "He ees rather handsome, is he not?"

Vixen!

"I suppose. Have you moved on from Pomeroy already?"

Miss Vasseur's pout deepened, and she made a show of dabbing at her large brown eyes, thick with mascara. "He is not even French. I feel like *une imbécile.*"

"He fooled us all, Estelle."

Miss Vasseur sniffed and threw her nose into the

air. "I believed he was pretending to be an earl. I heard the Gold family has money."

Miss Vasseur thought Charles was after Felicia's money? If she only knew.

"And now to learn he is a real earl? And that he did not come back to me. Do you know how humiliated I am?" She slapped her hands together as if ridding them of a distasteful substance. "I have finished with him, Harry. The silly little English *fille* can have him. And *bonne chance!*"

"That's my girl."

"I heard about Jean-Claude. So much bad luck. I will go back to Paris." Placing her chin on her fist, she stared out the window. Then she stiffened. "Ees that Pierre?"

Ginger risked a look. Both Miss Vasseur and Mr. Webster turned away from her as they looked out the window. The top of Mr. Dubois' head, his forehead, and his hat, rolled smoothly along the windows. He stopped when he reached Mr. Webster, then banged angrily on the window.

Mr. Webster laughed. "He's upset that I didn't lift his dead weight and that blasted chair into the café." He stretched and placed two hands on his lower back. "I'm sick of dragging him around like a sack of flour. It's killing me."

Miss Vasseur reached over and patted Mr. Webster's arm. "You are an excellent friend to him, Harry."

"Yes, well, he had a bad go of it in the war," Mr. Webster said. "It could've easily been me in that chair."

Miss Vasseur lowered her gaze. "You know, I did love him, once. And if it weren't for the chair—"

Ginger scowled inwardly. Miss Vassseur hadn't been married to Pierre Dubois, and had no obligations to him, but to abandon someone after he sacrificed so much, merely because he was consigned to a chair seemed heartless.

Mr. Webster stood to go. "So sorry for not drinking the tea, but my back is killing me." He stared at her hopefully. "Will you come to my flat later?" Then with that annoying grin he added, "I can make you forget Pomeroy."

Scoundrel!

Ginger was pleased when Miss Vasseur rejected his offer.

"Another time, then," he said casually before sauntering off.

Ginger slid, ungracefully, from her chair before Miss Vasseur left and made a point of making a fuss over Boss in Miss Vasseur's presence.

"*Un chien mignon,*" she said. "Your dog is sweet."

"Merci," Ginger returned. In French, she said, "I couldn't help overhearing that horrible man proposition you. Good for you for turning him away."

"I am used to piggy men like that."

"They came out in their dozens during the war years."

"So true," Miss Vasseur said. "You were in France?"

Ginger motioned to Mr. Webster's vacated chair. "Do you mind?"

"Not at all. Would you like some tea? He never touched his cup."

"I'm fine, thank you. I've had plenty already." After settling in the chair, she added, "To answer your question, yes, I was in France. I worked as a telephone operator."

"Those were terrible times," Miss Vasseur said. "We did what we had to do to survive."

Ginger leaned in and smiled. "It's just coming to me how I know you. Please forgive me, but were you at the wedding of the Earl of Witt?"

Miss Vasseur's genial demeanour evaporated. "Not exactly. But if you were there, then you saw me try to stop the charade. To me, he is Henri

Pomeroy. I thought he loved me. I guess I was wrong."

"I'm so sorry," Ginger said genuinely.

"No. But in the war, people were whatever they needed to be to ensure that the allies won." She forced a smile. "That is what I am telling myself, anyway."

"It's a good thing you missed the wedding reception," Ginger said. "There was a murder! Did you hear?"

"It is in all the papers. I find small comfort in it, as it turns out I knew the man who died."

"Such a shame," Ginger said. "How did you know him?"

"There was a group of soldiers who came to the public house in my town, and Jean-Claude was among them. The man you saw with me earlier was part of that group.

"So sad. Did you know anyone else at the wedding, besides the groom, that is?" Ginger asked.

Miss Vasseur stared out the window at Mr. Webster and Mr. Dubois in the distance, the former pushing the latter.

"Yes. That man in the chair," she said, pointing. "I loved him once too . . . when his legs worked. Before I met Pomeroy."

Charles!

Miss Vasseur must've read the displeasure on Ginger's face as she quickly added, "It wasn't like that. Pierre was missing for a long time. Everyone thought he was dead. I sought comfort—"

"Yes, no sense in belabouring the point, Mademoiselle—"

"Vasseur."

"I am acquainted with Mr. Hughes, who is also a good friend of the groom. Do you know him as well?"

"A little bit," Miss Vasseur said. She leaned in and raised a brow. "But I'd like to get to know him better. Handsome and with money, I hear. Do you know, is he yet single?"

Ginger doubted Miss Vasseur's story, that she hadn't known that Henri Pomeroy and the Earl of Witt were the same person. She clearly was looking to marry a man of means.

"I regret to say that I am not privy to that kind of information," Ginger replied as she rose to her feet. She tugged on Boss' leash, and her pet came to her side. "Mademoiselle Vasseur, it's been a pleasure."

"Wait," Miss Vasseur called as Ginger stepped away. "I did not get your name."

Ginger paused. "Mademoiselle LaFleur."

Miss Vasseur's eyes widened as they settled on Ginger's stomach. Ginger had momentarily forgotten about that. By rights, she should've said Madame, not Mademoiselle. Oh well. It wasn't as if Miss Vasseur was a stranger to scandal.

According to Miss Ward's statement, she lived in Notting Hill. As the second female associated with this case, Ginger felt it prudent to call in on Miss Ward for a second interview. Ginger hadn't believed Miss Vasseur to be genuinely in love with Charles, and she suspected Miss Ward's performance of grief over Jean-Claude Beaulieu as well. Miss Ward was an actress and a convincing one, it would appear.

Ginger nearly ran into a tree as she parked her Crossley in front of Miss Ward's residence. Perhaps she touched it with her bumper, but neither the bumper nor the tree was injured, so there was nothing to concern herself over.

"Come along, Boss," she said. She walked with

Boss on his leash, and just as she was about to step off the pavement to the front door, she caught sight of a familiar green Austin 7. She smiled as she watched Basil climb out.

"Great minds think alike," she said.

Basil's smile was stiff. "I thought you were resting?"

"I was. But then I got inspired."

Basil's shoulders relaxed in defeat. "There's no keeping you down, is there, Mrs. Reed?"

"No, there's not, so you might as well stop trying. I just had an interesting cup of tea." Ginger proceeded to fill him in on the conversation she'd had with Miss Vasseur, minus the last bit about her own fake name.

"Webster and Dubois?" Basil said with a note of surprise. "I just interviewed them at a hotel bar in Belgravia. I had to go back to the Yard for a bit, then I headed here."

"That explains Mr. Webster's apparent state of intoxication," Ginger said. "Rather early in the day."

"Webster spoke somewhat unkindly about Miss Ward. I thought it merited a second interview. Why are you here?"

"Oh, just intuition."

Basil gave her a sideways glance but let it go at

that. They entered the building in search of flat number six, found on the floor above. As Basil knocked, Ginger wondered if they were on a fool's errand. They had no reason to believe Miss Ward would be home in the afternoon, but as luck would have it, she opened the door.

"Oh?" she said with a note of disappointment. Dressed in a simple day frock and wearing little make-up, she was hardly recognisable as the flamboyant mistress of Jean-Claude Beaulieu Ginger had met at the wedding reception.

"Were you expecting someone else?" Basil asked.

"I'm running out of coal for my fire. I was hoping it was the delivery man."

"We're still investigating the death of Mr. Beaulieu," Basil continued. "Would you mind if we asked you a few more questions?"

Miss Ward waved them inside. Her flat contained all the essentials—a living room with a connected kitchen—yet one would find it challenging to sit, as clothing was strewn about the place.

"I hope you don't mind that I have my little dog?" Ginger said. "He's very well behaved."

Miss Ward shrugged. "It's not like he could make the place messier." Then, as if to explain the chaotic condition of her flat, she added, "I have an audition later, and I'm trying to decide what to wear."

Miss Ward swooped up an armful of clothing from the sofa so Ginger and Basil could sit.

"The play's called *Easy Virtue*," she said. " It was all the rage in New York. Have you seen it? I'm trying for the part of the glamorous divorcée." She discarded the garments onto another chair. "Jean-Claude's death devastated me, but a girl has to eat." She pulled up a kitchen chair, sat, and crossed her legs. "I wish I could lounge around in my grief, but I don't have that luxury."

"We'll be quick about it," Basil said. "How long were you and Mr. Beaulieu, er, associated?"

"Over three years. If only . . . I might be engaged to be married right now, instead of worrying about my next role."

Ginger watched as Miss Ward kept her hands busy and eyes averted. "What is your relationship to Mr. Webster?"

Miss Ward stiffened. She caught Ginger's gaze. "I don't know what you mean. I don't have a relationship with Mr. Webster."

"That's not what he said," Basil replied.

Miss Ward glared. "Then he's a liar!"

"Is he?" Ginger asked gently. "It's not unusual for a lady to love more than one man in her life.

Miss Ward let out a long breath then lowered herself onto a chair, despite the clothing strewn across it. "All right, fine. I loved Harry once, but he's not the sort of man to settle on one girl, and not the sort of man I would want to marry."

"You wanted to marry Jean-Claude?" Ginger asked.

"Yes."

Basil leaned forward. "But he didn't want to marry you, did he, Miss Ward?"

Miss Ward sobbed, grabbing the nearest blouse draped over the arm of the chair and pressing it to her eyes. "Why would you say such a thing?"

"Did he ask you to join him in the garden?" Basil asked. "You believed he was about to propose, and when he refused, were you angry enough to kill him?"

Miss Ward jumped to her feet. "No! It wasn't like that. I didn't kill him!"

"What *really* happened last night?" Ginger asked.

"It's true, we argued in the garden, but he was alive when I left him, I swear. I went straight to the cloakroom and gathered my coat."

"What did you argue about?" Basil asked.

With an exaggerated rolling of her eyes, Miss Ward said, "I thought he was going to propose, but he only wanted to scrounge a cigarette."

"Why did you tell us that Mr. Beaulieu was with you in the entrance hall?" Ginger asked.

"Because I knew how it would look. That you'd think me a killer like you clearly now do." Her eyes were glassy as she pleaded. "It wasn't me. I left Jean-Claude in the garden, hoping that he'd run after me. It's why I waited around. And then the gunshot—"

Her knees gave out, and she slumped back onto the piles of clothes.

"Did anyone see you leave the garden?" Ginger asked.

Miss Ward sat up and held Ginger's gaze. "Yes, as a matter of fact. Mr. Dubois saw me. The door to the study leading to the corridor was open. You can ask him."

Ginger shared a look with Basil, who lifted a shoulder, then stood. It appeared neither of them had further questions for the actress.

Basil held a hand to Ginger, helping her to her feet, then turned to Miss Ward. "Thank you for your time, Miss Ward. We will do as you ask and confirm your alibi with Mr. Dubois." He set his hat on his head then added, "In the meantime, please don't leave London without speaking to the police first."

After leaving Miss Ward, Ginger returned to Hartigan House, where she and Basil met up again in time for dinner. Mrs. Beasley had outdone herself with a meal of roast duck, followed by blackberry and apple pie. Ambrosia and Scout were present for the affair, but Ginger found she sought Felicia's empty seat with longing. How she already missed Felicia! Her absence in the house was like a vacant echo. It reminded Ginger of when her friend Haley Higgins had gone back to Boston, and how she always expected to see her tall friend with her head of curly brown hair when she entered the sitting room in the evenings to share the highlights of their day. Eventually, Ginger stopped looking for Haley and though she still missed her, had found her footing without her.

At least Felicia would remain in the city, and she'd even asked if she could still call into the office of Lady Gold Investigations and help occasionally.

Ginger's end-of-day winding down in the sitting room happened with Basil now. She sighed content-edly as she leaned against him as they reclined together on the rose-coloured settee. One of Ginger's new maids had started a fire which crackled and shed warm light on the room. The curtains, now drawn, covered the tall windows.

"Poor Felicia is desperate to leave on her wedding journey to Greece," Ginger started, "and I don't blame her."

Basil sipped his brandy. "We can't keep Charles and Felicia forever. Hopefully, we'll get to the bottom of this case soon." He sighed as he kissed Ginger's head. "Not every case is solved."

"Oh, we must solve this one, or it will be a cloud over the memories of Felicia's happy day forever." Ginger had exchanged brandy for tea once she'd discovered she was with child and carefully took a sip. "We hardly even have a prime suspect."

"Harry Webster is an interesting candidate," Basil said. "Perhaps the two men duelled over Miss Ward."

"Mr. Webster hardly seems the type to kill over a lady. I have the feeling he's had his pick over the years. Besides, according to Mr. Webster and Miss Ward, our victim wasn't interested in securing Miss Ward as his wife. He'd hardly give his life for the cause."

"Then Miss Ward," Basil offered. "Her tears are

convincing, but I've learned from experience that a woman's emotional demonstrations can't be trusted."

Ginger bristled, hoping he was referring to his late wife and not to her.

Seeming to read Ginger's mind, Basil gently placed a lock of her red bob behind her ear. "You, dear, have only been wonderfully transparent."

Ginger felt guilt now, as she knew that wasn't true, either.

"Miss Ward has motive and opportunity," Ginger said. "But how would she have got her hands on Charles' old pistol?"

Basil cleared his throat. "We don't know that Miss Ward and Charles hadn't been previously acquainted."

"Oh mercy. I do hope you're wrong." However, Charles had been involved with Miss Vasseur. A dalliance with Miss Ward wouldn't be beyond the realms of possibility.

Thinking of Miss Vasseur, she said, "Estelle Vasseur is a dark horse. The way she made a scene at the wedding and then a man is murdered that same night."

"Were she and Beaulieu acquainted?"

"They were," Ginger confirmed. "When I approached her at the tearoom, she said so. She knew all the men in question." She shifted in her seat and threw an arm into the air as she stretched and yawned. "I feel like we're missing something, Basil. Something so obvious we can't see it."

Basil helped her to her feet and embraced her. "Perhaps if you slept on it, love, it would come to you."

Never liking to be left out, Boss stirred in his little bed by the hearth. He whined as he stretched his belly low to the floor then trotted over to join their huddle. Ginger laughed. "What do you think, Bossy? Shall we sleep on it? Will we find the killer in our dreams?"

$\mathcal{A}$ soft tapping on the bedroom door caused Basil's eyes to snap open. Not disturbing Ginger, he carefully sat up and listened intently. The tapping returned. He eased his legs over the side of the bed and slid his bare feet into his slippers. His dressing gown hung on the bedpost, and he slid his arms into the sleeves and tied the robe at his waist with the fabric belt. He cracked open the door to find Pippins, dressed similarly in his nightshirt and robe, with the addition of a nightcap on his bald head and a dripping candle in a brass holder in his hand.

Basil stepped into the corridor. "Pippins," he said quietly. "What is it?"

"So sorry to disturb you, sir," the older man said,

"but Constable Braxton rang from Scotland Yard. He wishes for you to ring him back. Apparently, it's rather urgent."

"Thank you, Pippins. You may return to your sleep."

Basil used a torch to make his way down the staircase and through the entrance hall—no sense turning on the electric lights just for himself—and to Ginger's study at the back of the house. There he switched on the electric lights, dialled the operator, and asked for the Yard.

"Reed here."

"Oh, jolly good," came Braxton's voice. "The super wanted me to ring you."

"What have you got, Braxton?"

"I'm afraid it's another body. The interloper at the wedding, Miss Estelle Vasseur."

Basil sighed. "Where?"

"At Witt House."

"How extraordinary," Basil said, wondering at all the coincidences. "I'll head over."

"I'll meet you there, sir."

Upstairs again, Basil tiptoed about the bedroom like a cat burglar. He selected trousers, a shirt, and a pair of socks. Ginger had so much difficulty sleeping well these days; he didn't want to risk waking her. After changing in the bathroom at the end of the corridor, he made his way to the back entrance of the house, where his coat and hat hung on a rack.

The torch came in handy as he passed the darkened kitchen, went out the door to the back garden, and walked down the path to the garage. He jumped into his Austin, and it sprang to life when he turned the key and engaged the engine. He was glad that their bedroom windows faced Mallowan Court, so his stealth exit didn't rouse Ginger. Belatedly, he considered that he should've left her a note, but at least Pippins knew about the call from Scotland Yard.

Travelling through London in the predawn hours was an entirely different experience from a daylight tour with the hustle and bustle of traffic— motorised and with four legs—and pedestrians all in a hurry to get somewhere. Now, there was peace and calm with only a few horses and carts moving about. The bakeries' lights dimly lit the streets.

Several police motorcars were at Charles' house when Basil arrived, and he wondered if the man had been notified. What a blasted string of misfortunes for this newlywed couple. Too many to be coincidence, but blast it all, he hated to believe Felicia's new husband, a man Basil regarded as a brother-in-law now, could be so devious and unfeeling as to act out murderous plots during his nuptials.

However, it could be precisely why he would. People were reluctant to suspect him, and his new wife could provide him with needed alibis, whether they were airtight or not.

Stepping out of the Austin, Basil adjusted his hat and searched for signs of activity. He noticed movement in the stairwell that led to the basement, recognising the rounded helmet belonging to a police officer in uniform. Under the brightness of the streetlights, he headed over.

"Sir!" Braxton said when he spotted him. "Over here." He pointed to the small wrought-iron gate that stood ajar, leading to the stairwell with an entrance to the basement.

Basil joined Braxton and saw that Newman was with him. "You lads cursed with the night shift, eh?" he said.

"Someone's got to do it, sir," Newman said solemnly. He pointed to the body on the steps. "She's there, sir."

A female with short dark hair lay at the bottom

of the stairwell that led to the basement. She wore a winter coat, but her cloche had fallen off in an apparent struggle, her arm twisted at an odd angle.

"Who reported it?" Basil asked.

Braxton answered, "Mr. Hughes, sir. Says he couldn't sleep and stepped outside for a walk and a cigarette. He saw her from his position on the step."

Basil crouched to examine the body without touching it. Scanning it with his torch beam, he could see blood pooling under the neck. A red line reached to one ear. "Her neck has been slit. Has the pathologist been rung?"

"Yes, sir," Newman replied.

Basil scoured the area with his torch then ran it over the body once again. Miss Vasseur's hands were in fists, and from this angle, it appeared that a piece of paper was crumpled up in one of them. He removed a pen from his pocket, squatted again, and worked open the fingers until he could pinch the corner of the bit of paper with his gloved hands. Smoothing it out, he read, "M.H."

"I think we need to have another chat with Mr. Hughes," he said, straightening.

Basil found Maximillian Hughes drinking whisky and smoking cigarettes in the sitting room. A newly lit fire ablaze in the stone fireplace cast flickering light and shadows.

"Have a seat, my good man," Hughes said with a wave of his arm. "I'm sure you have questions, and I'm equally sure I don't have the answers." He raised his glass. "Care for a drink? Compliments of the groom!"

Basil shook his head. "It's either too early or too late; I'm not sure which. Either way, I'm on the job now."

"Yes, of course." Hughes took a long sip of his whisky and sighed over the burn. "Two bodies in so many days. I'd call that unlucky."

"What was your relationship to Miss Vasseur?"

Hughes' head jerked. "Miss Estelle Vasseur? She's the dead woman?"

"I was told you were the one to call the police," Basil said. "Did you not recognise her?"

"She was lying face down, so no."

"Then, if you don't mind answering my original question, Mr. Hughes."

"I have no relationship with her whatsoever."

"Are you saying you're not acquainted?"

Hughes' lips pulled slightly. "We're acquainted in that I met her once. In Belgium, as it were." He lowered his chin, now darkened with growth, and looked at Basil. "She was on the arm of my host."

"Davenport-Witt," Basil said to confirm.

Hughes grinned. "The one and only."

Basil frowned. Naturally, Charles knew the layout of his own house. No, he refused to believe the man vile enough to marry, simply to commit a murder. Besides, had Charles wanted Beaulieu dead, he could've gone about it in several ways and with less attention given to the event. And certainly, the same would be true for Miss Vasseur.

"How long have you been staying as Davenport-Witt's guest?" Basil asked.

"A week or so. I prefer London. More to do to keep oneself entertained than what Cardiff has to offer."

"That seems rather generous of Charles."

"Yes, well, I suppose you could say he's in my debt."

"How so?" Basil asked.

Hughes snorted. "I hardly know what that would have to do with this."

"Perhaps nothing. I won't know until I hear it, and I don't have to remind you that you're now implicated in two deaths."

Hughes puffed on his cigarette then blew smoke

rings into the air. "Very well. He'd learned that Pierre Dubois had been found alive."

"Ah," Basil said with a nod. "And he was entangled with Miss Vassuer, Mr. Dubois' former love."

"Yes. Davenport-Witt wanted to end things with Miss Vasseur, out of respect for Dubois, but she was very reluctant to give him up."

"How do you fit in with things?"

"I intercepted her as he sneaked out of town. She was rather persistent, and Davenport-Witt didn't want to create a scene."

After her performance at the wedding ceremony, Basil believed the lady was the persistent type.

"That was good of you," Basil said, "but hardly a favour one would hold over another man's head."

"There was more to it. Dubois had got wind of the affair. Davenport-Witt asked me to convince him that he'd never been involved with Miss Vasseur, to blame it on a mystery man. Webster helped to create the illusion. In fact—" Hughes lowered his chin and looked pointedly at Basil. "Webster is very devoted to Dubois."

"What do you mean by that?"

"Only that Webster is the kind of fellow who takes on the offence of others."

"Are you suggesting Webster might perform acts of revenge on behalf of his friend?"

"I doubt it. I just want to point out that I'm not your only suspect."

Basil bucked at the suggestion he wasn't doing a thorough job. "Did the ruse with Webster work? Did Dubois believe Webster's story about the mystery man?"

Hughes lifted a shoulder. "Dubois was on a lot of pain medication. In the end, I don't think he knew up from down, much less the truth about Miss Vasseur."

"Why did Miss Vasseur call Davenport-Witt Pomeroy?"

A long pause was followed by a puff of his cigarette and a slurp of whisky. "I hardly know how to answer that," he finally said. "Female hysteria, perhaps?"

"As of right now, you are without an alibi for either death, Mr. Hughes," Basil said. "Tell me why I shouldn't take you down to the station."

Mr. Hughes refilled his whisky glass. "I will tell you in confidence. My alibi can be found in this house, amongst the staff."

"Are you suggesting an assignation?"

"You've met the pretty little maid, Daphne?"

"Oh, good heavens."

Mr. Hughes took a large drink then sighed with the heat of the whisky going down. "I'm not proud of it, Chief Inspector. But she's one reason I've been hanging about. If you must ask her, go ahead, but I do hope you can spare the poor thing the humiliation."

Leaving through the front door, Basil watched as the body of Miss Vasseur was removed. He'd been focused entirely on the stairwell, imagining the rendezvous that had been appointed there, so he hadn't yet taken stock of the two steps leading to the front door. A thin mat lay on the step, the kind made of thick jute intended to catch dust and dirt from one's shoes before going inside. It looked awfully new, not to be unexpected in preparation for a wedding, yet it failed to show the slightest signs of wear, and there had been a sizable number of people traipsing in and out.

Basil squatted, picked the mat up by one corner, and worked his lips. Brown splatters marred the underside of the mat, and he expected the laboratory would confirm his suspicions. Blood. Undoubtedly belonging to Miss Vasseur. Whoever killed the lady had surprised her on the front doorstep then conveniently pushed her over the low wrought-iron railing into the stairwell. The killer hadn't expected the blood that would escape the body before it could be "relocated" and had quickly concealed the evidence by flipping the mat.

Both Hughes and Webster were looking guilty. Basil just needed to work out which one was a murderer.

Ginger thought little about Basil's side of the bed being empty when she awoke, as he often rose earlier than she did, especially as her pregnancy had progressed, but she was a little surprised to find he wasn't in the breakfast room when she got there.

She called for Pippins. "Have you seen Mr. Reed about the house?"

"No, madam. He left before dawn this morning."

"Whatever for?"

"Scotland Yard rang for him, madam, and he left shortly afterwards. I'm afraid that's all I know."

Oh mercy. Whatever it was must've been urgent for Basil to leave at that hour. Ginger couldn't help but feel a little distressed that he hadn't bothered to wake her. She supposed he valued her sleep over rousing her to get ready to come along, but now, her curiosity was making her nerves jump.

"Thank you, Pips," she said. Heading straight for the study, she dialled the operator and asked to be connected to the Yard. Thankfully, Basil was there to take her call.

"I'm sorry, love," he said. "I was in such a hurry; I forgot to leave a note."

"What was so urgent that you had to jump out of bed in the middle of the night?"

"I'm afraid there's been another murder."

Ginger not only felt distressed but also alarmed as Basil broke the news of Miss Vasseur's demise.

"I'm so sorry to hear that. Do you know what happened?"

"Dr. Gupta examined the body at the scene. Someone cut Miss Vasseur's throat."

"Any evidence of note?"

"There was a scrap of paper in her fist. A small bit, as if the rest of the note had been ripped from her hand. The initials M.H. were scribbled on it."

"Maximillian Hughes," Ginger offered. "What did he have to say for himself?"

There was a pause on the other side, and for a moment, Ginger thought they'd been cut off. But then Basil answered, "He was very close-lipped for someone who was in the vicinity of two murders in the last two days. All I know is that there is a connection between Miss Vasseur, Hughes, Dubois, Webster, Beaulieu, and Davenport-Witt."

Ginger hated to include Charles, but he'd admitted to being in Witt House when the shot went off, to collect Felicia's forgotten handbag. "I agree."

Another pause was followed by a sigh from Basil. "Ginger, if you know something that could help me . . ."

Ginger heard the challenge in Basil's voice. Over the last while, they'd come to an uneasy truce. Basil suspected Ginger's involvement in a clandestine organization, and she did nothing to discourage him from thinking so. Still, she'd never admitted to it openly nor broken her vow of secrecy. To Basil's credit, he never pushed the matter or tried to force her. Still, when it came up, it was an unpleasant marker that their relationship wasn't completely open and honest. This was a deep regret for Ginger, but alas, she was stuck between the proverbial rock and a hard place.

Basil wanted to know if she was aware of classified information that would help him solve these murders, which she was. But how could she help her husband and keep her oath? Would her silence let a guilty man go free?

She answered without answering at all. "I'm sure if we put our heads together, we can solve this. Let me think on it longer."

"Very well," Basil said, but Ginger could hear the disappointment in his voice. "What do you think about Harry Webster?"

"As a prime suspect?" Ginger said. "He's just as much a possibility as the others. He had the opportunity, and if he was the one to steal Charles' pistol, he had the means. What of motive?"

"Hughes suggested he might work as an avenger for Dubois."

"Acting as his legs?"

"Precisely."

"Although—" a new prospect formed in Ginger's mind.

"Yes?"

"You said M.H. was written on the scrap of paper found in Miss Vasseur's hand. Is it possible you read it upside down? Could it be H. W.?"

Ginger heard rustling on the end of the line and assumed Basil was retrieving the bit of evidence. "By golly, Ginger, I think you're onto something. I had Hughes on the brain."

"The note could very well have been intended for Mr. Hughes," Ginger said. "Miss Vasseur indicated an interest in getting acquainted with him."

"Perhaps it wasn't meant to be a romantic rendezvous with Mr. Hughes, but the settling of affairs."

"Are you suggesting that she had damaging information about H.W.?" Ginger asked. "And that Mr. Webster took matters into his own hands?"

"Anything is possible at this point. What are your plans today, should I need to find you?"

"I think I'll stay at home today. I'm feeling rather tired from all the commotion. Putting my feet up with a cup of tea and a book is exactly what I need."

"Good idea," Basil said, his relief reaching her through the wire. "I'll be home for dinner. After I question Harry Webster."

Ginger slowly returned the black receiver to its cradle. Harry Webster could have committed both murders. He appeared to be very protective of his pal Pierre and perhaps had been driven to exact vengeance on behalf of his friend who was unable to do it himself.

She opened the desk drawer to remove her old journal. She flipped through the pages, looking for the entry that was flickering in her mind.

February 1, 1917

Pantin

Pantin, the French operative who'd been captured by the Germans two weeks ago, was rescued. Unconscious and gravely wounded, he'd been left to die in a shelled outbuilding near Maubeuge. He'd been discovered by one of our own, who'd crossed enemy lines to search for him. Miraculously, he smuggled Pantin back into unoccupied France.

I rushed to the triage centre in Amiens, a church with the pews removed, where I found Pantin propped against the metal back of his hospital bed and staring out the window onto the snowy fields that lay just behind the hospital. His beard had been shaved off, and his head and one side of his face were covered in bandages. He had never been large and had easily lost at least a stone, maybe more, making him look more like a frail lad than a man. His right arm was in a cast, and his chest was also bandaged. Both his legs were in casts.

I pulled up one of the wooden chairs and sat beside him. We conversed in French.

"Oh, it is you, Mademoiselle LaFleur." His

voice was raspy from disuse and perhaps from trauma to his neck, which appeared bruised.

"It's good to see you again," I returned.

"Besides Webster, who saved me, you are the only one to visit me. Other than the hospital staff, no one has come to me."

"I'm sure Captain Smithwick is on his way or will be when he's told you're alive. I'm not sure where he is now, though."

"Did they tell you I was in a coma until two days ago?"

"Yes. What do you remember?"

"I remember the Boche came before we could accomplish our mission and that I—" He glanced away, looking ashamed.

"It's not your fault, Pantin. If anyone is to blame, it is Captain Smithwick." I'd expressed my concern about the nearby German garrison, but he'd brushed me off and pushed the operation through.

"I can be thankful I'd hit my head," Pantin said, "and that even when they slapped me around, I was unconscious most of the time and unable to tell them anything."

He swallowed with difficulty, and I helped him sip tepid water from a glass.

"I would be dead right now if it weren't for *Araignée*."

Spider.

I know him now as Harry Webster. Spider's nickname was an old one from his childhood and derived from his last name, but few knew that. We'd thought he'd been killed, but despite breaking his nose in the attack, he'd actually gone back for his friend.

"What else do you remember?"

Pantin sighed. "After I was captured, they took me to the garrison in Jemappes. They didn't waste any time interrogating me. I don't know if they had other prisoners, but they seemed to enjoy focusing on me." He raised his good arm and pointed to his left cheek. "They started here, with a knife."

Oh mercy!

"They ask me who my compatriots are; what are the names of my superiors." He stopped for a moment and looked at me. "I pretended to be out of my mind. I told them nothing."

I let out a long breath. His silence had, without question, saved lives.

"Then they started on my ribs with their rifle butts. Two are broken," He looked down at his legs, "Then one of them started on my legs. The doctor tells me I may never walk again."

I felt anger rising in me.

"After a while, I passed out for real. In the middle of the night, I awoke in a dark cell in great pain. I lay there for a time. It is hard to tell how long, maybe four hours. When you are in agony, time goes slowly."

Carefully, I placed a hand on his arm. "I regret you had to go through this, Pantin."

"Just as I was begging God to take me, I heard scratching, and there was Spider. He picked me up and carried me out into the forest. I do not know how he did it, but he found a horse and wagon. It was a long, painful ride, mademoiselle, and I passed out several times. The next thing I remember, I was in this bed with bandages and casts and a constant need for morphine."

A nurse had recently given him a shot of the medication, and it had kicked in. "Tell Estelle I'm here, will you? Will you?"

I didn't know who Estelle was, but as I squeezed his hand, I said, "I will."

Ginger remembered the triage room like she'd been there yesterday. Beds filled the nave, one after the other, the groans and coughing of ill and injured men echoing through the lofty ceilings. The smell was strong and unpleasant, a mix of mould, bleach, and sickness. Her promise to Pantin was an offer of false hope. She hadn't found Estelle Vasseur.

She picked up the receiver again and asked the operator to connect her to Charles' residence. When the butler answered, she said, "I'd like to leave a message for Mr. Pierre Dubois."

Ginger rang the bell that sounded in the kitchen, and soon Lizzie appeared at her study door. She offered a slight curtsey.

"Yes, madam? How can I be of service?"

"I've invited a guest for a cup of tea. Mr. Dubois uses a wheelchair, so please inform Clement that he will require help."

"Yes, madam. Would you like refreshments brought to the sitting room?"

"That would be splendid, thank you."

Ginger had failed to eat breakfast, and with a loud growl, her stomach made its protest known. She spent the time waiting for Mr. Dubois' arrival availing herself of the food laid out in the morning room.

Ambrosia looked up as Ginger entered and set a half-empty teacup on its saucer. "Mrs. Schofield has insisted I go for tea this morning," she said.

Mrs. Schofield didn't take Ambrosia's station in life as seriously as Ambrosia did and was thus a thorn in her flesh where propriety was concerned. It was that same dedication to decency that kept Ambrosia from declining the invitation.

"I'm going to listen to some music in the drawing room to calm my nerves before I fulfil my social obligations."

After passing Ginger's request on to Clement, Lizzie returned with a fresh pot of tea.

"Has Scout eaten already?" Ginger asked. She'd been so consumed with Basil's late-night escapade, and the subsequent rabbit trails, that she'd not even noticed. Again, she felt guilty of poor mothering and patted her stomach.

"Yes, madam. He's left with Mr. Fulton on a field trip. Mrs. Beasley provided a picnic lunch. They've taken Boss with them."

It took a village to raise a child, and Ginger was grateful she'd found such an excellent tutor for Scout in Mr. Fulton.

Having eaten her fill, Ginger returned upstairs to her room and settled on her dressing table chair. Her reflection proved that she'd got older since the war. Wrinkles had formed around her eyes where there once were none, and she'd even plucked out the odd white hair occasionally. Her red hair was much shorter and easier to hide under hats, especially the cloche-style ones all the rage. Still, she'd been hatless at the wedding reception, and Mr. Dubois had proved he'd recognised her with his jab about Mademoiselle LaFleur.

A closer look in the mirror showed a few stray eyebrow hairs marring the deep, thin arches, and she expertly plucked the strays. She waited for her eyes to stop watering before adding blue shadow on the lids and finishing with mascara. Her well-used mascara pad and brush set needed replacing, and she made a mental note to add them to her shopping list.

Ginger brushed her bob and used decorative pins to pin it off her forehead.

Lizzie knocked on the door, just in time, to help her select a day dress. With her growing stomach, Ginger's choices were more limited, and Lizzie's help in getting into and out of them was appreciated.

She selected a simple day frock of burgundy canton crepe with contrasting tones and glinting metal threads in the skirt. The long sleeves were cuffed and matched the square collar. An examination in the full-length mirror confirmed she'd made the right choice. She wasn't sure what she expected from her meeting with Mr. Dubois, but it never hurt for one to look one's best.

The front bell's musical tone sounded through the house, even reaching her bedroom. In the corridor, yet out of sight, Ginger waited for Pippins to answer the door. After some commotion as Clement rolled Mr. Dubois inside the house, Pippins took over and wheeled the man to the sitting room. Ginger waited an appropriate amount of time then headed down to greet her guest.

She'd only made it to the entrance hall when she heard Felicia's voice coming from the back of the house. *Drat! What blasted terrible timing!*

"Oh, Ginger, there you are! I hope you don't mind; I got Charles to drop me off. It seems Basil wanted to see him at the Yard, for who knows what, so I thought I might as well spend some time with you!"

"Darling," Ginger said, "you're always welcome, but I've just received a guest."

"Oh? Who?"

"Mr. Dubois. You can join us for tea if you like."

Felicia cocked her head. "I didn't know that you and Mr. Dubois were acquainted."

"It seems we met during the war. His memory is better than mine, but I thought I should be hospitable before he heads back to France."

"Forgive me, but I find reminiscing about the war to be frightfully boring. I get quite enough of that from Charles. I was too young to appreciate it for what it was, I'm afraid."

"That's all right," Ginger said with relief. "Why don't you go and see your grandmother. I believe she's in the drawing room."

Ginger watched as Felicia walked to the opposite side of the entrance hall and pushed through the heavy wooden door that opened to the drawing room. Then Ginger stepped into the sitting room. A fire was going in the fireplace, and a setting for tea was on the coffee table. One armchair beside the settee was pulled out of position, and in its place sat Pierre Dubois, looking worse for wear.

She sat on one end of the settee and smiled. "Hello, Pantin."

CHAPTER TWENTY

Like master chess players, Basil faced Lord Davenport-Witt, who sat on the opposite side of Basil's desk at Scotland Yard, and waited for the next move. Only, the game they played was one of the mind, rather than on a board with movable pieces.

"So kind of you to come in, Charles, and at short notice," Basil said. "Fancy a drink?"

Davenport-Witt grinned as he casually crossed his legs. "At the Yard's expense?"

"The quality you get here, tea of course, is hardly expensive, but I do keep a bottle of whisky in my drawer for special occasions."

"I'm flattered to be found special," Davenport-Witt said. "I'll take you up on it, if you'll join me."

Basil opened the lower drawer on the left side of his desk and produced a bottle, three-quarters full, and two glasses. He rarely drank in his office, preferring Ginger's company and a glass of brandy at the end of the day, but the ruse was known by all on the force as a tactic to loosen the tongue. He poured both glasses two fingers deep, intending to slowly sip his own.

Davenport-Witt pleased him by taking a long swig. After letting out a long breath noting his appreciation of the beverage, he settled his gaze on Basil. "So, old chap, do tell me why I'm here."

"Can't one offer an invitation to a new groom?" Basil said. "We're practically related now."

"Most assuredly, though one would think a club or lounge might be preferable to a small office tucked away at Scotland Yard."

"You're right." Basil nodded with his chin at the dimly lit room, sparsely furnished with just a desk, a couple of chairs, and a row of filing cabinets. "This is hardly suitable. I suggest we meet again in the future and celebrate properly."

"However—"

"However, I would like to ask you a few questions about your wedding guests."

"Finally, to the point. We English certainly do like to beat around the bush, don't we?"

"Indeed."

Davenport-Witt shifted in his chair and recrossed his legs in the other direction. "Very well, ask away."

"Mr. Hughes is a person of interest. You know him well. Did he have a reason to kill either of our victims? Mr. Beaulieu or Miss Vasseur?"

"It grieves me that Max is under suspicion, Chief Inspector. I can attest to his character. Though not without fault, he's hardly a murderer."

Using a common interrogation technique, Basil swiftly changed gears. "Charles, I can't recall if I've asked this before, but did you and my wife meet on the continent during the war?"

All expression left Davenport-Witt's face; a phenomenon Basil had witnessed in Ginger many times when he'd broach certain subjects. It was like a window slamming closed, and though one could see the eyes, the clarity of vision was dulled.

Basil's conviction that there was an unofficial government agency at work was only growing. He'd suspected his wife's involvement for some time, though not due to any fault of hers. Others they had encountered in the course of their joint investigations had shed light on areas of Ginger's mystique.

Ginger was the kind of person who always believed the best of someone, especially if they were a new acquaintance, but her regard for Davenport-Witt was the exception. From the day they had encountered the man on their holiday in Brighton, she'd exhibited uncharacteristic suspicion towards him.

Basil couldn't help wonder if she'd met Davenport-Witt before, during the war.

A slight twitch of the man's lips was the only clue Basil had that his guest might be preparing to lie.

"I'm not sure what you're driving at here, old chap," Davenport-Witt said, "but to ease your curiosity, I'll answer. In a word, no. If we met, I don't remember it now. I'll admit, when I first saw her with Felicia in the hotel lobby in Brighton, I thought she looked familiar. But all redheads tend to look alike."

Basil couldn't keep the shock of that statement from registering on his face, and Davenport-Witt laughed. "Oh, do forgive me. Mrs. Reed is certainly an exception. At least to you."

"How do you know Mr. Webster and Mr.

Dubois?" Basil asked, pivoting again. "From what I can ascertain, you rarely crossed paths in the war."

Davenport-Witt shot back the rest of his whisky. "Not all friendships were forged in battle, Basil, as you would know if you'd lasted."

Basil ignored the dig. He'd been invalided out of the war in his first combat, with a constant dull ache in his side where his spleen had once lived as a constant reminder. How Davenport-Witt had become party to this personal information, Basil didn't know. Perhaps Felicia had revealed it.

Basil pursed his lips. "You haven't answered the question."

"I met Webster in Paris during a shared time of leave. I knew Dubois was a friend of his, and for this reason I invited him to my wedding."

"That was very generous of you," Basil said wryly.

"I like to think I'm a generous man. But, in this case, perhaps too generous." Davenport-Witt uncrossed his legs and leaned in. "If you're looking for a man capable of murder, I'd look to Dubois."

Basil raised a brow. "A man in a wheelchair?"

Davenport-Witt leaned back in his chair. "True, that is somewhat problematic."

There was a tap on the door and following Basil's instructions to enter, Braxton stepped in. "Telephone call for you, sir," he said. "A message from Mr. Pippins. You're to go to Hartigan House immediately. It's urgent."

"Hello, Mademoiselle LaFleur." Pierre Dubois laughed heartily. "Zee sings zee war turned us into. Liars, cheaters, deceivers." He slapped his legs. "Invalids."

"The whole thing was a dreadful affair, turning humans into monsters. It's hard for some of us to revert to who we were before the war."

Mr. Dubois ducked his chin. "What are you implying?"

Instead of answering, Ginger said, slipping into French, "Tea?" She held up the pot and poured. "Milk and sugar?"

Mr. Dubois replied in French as well. "I'd prefer coffee, but if that's not on offer, tea will suffice."

"I could provide coffee if you don't mind waiting."

"Please don't trouble yourself," Mr. Dubois said, then accepted the floral teacup and matching saucer. "But you must answer my question. Who amongst us is the monster?"

"If we knew that," Ginger said after a careful sip, "we'd have our killer."

"Witty connivers too."

"What do you mean?"

"The war has made us into that as well."

Ginger hummed. "I was thinking about the time I visited you in triage at the church. Do you remember the occasion?"

"Vaguely. Webster was incensed. But you, Mrs. Reed, were as cool as a cucumber."

"It was a coping mechanism, I assure you. You and Mr. Webster became good friends during the war and appear to have remained so to this day."

"Yes. I suppose one good thing has come of it."

Ginger laid her teacup down. "I'm afraid I have unpleasant news, Mr. Dubois. The police have taken Mr. Webster in for questioning."

Scowling, Mr. Dubois snapped, "What on earth for?"

"The murders of Mr. Beaulieu and Miss Vasseur."

He snorted. "The incompetence of the Metropolitan Police is astounding. Is this why you invited me here?" he growled. "To get me out of the way so your pompous husband could make a fool of himself by arresting the wrong man?"

Ginger ignored the insult directed at her husband, though she wouldn't deny it irked her. "If Mr. Webster is the wrong man, who is the right one?"

"How would I know? I am not the police. But if I had my legs, I would do a better job than them. I would detain your beloved earl, for one."

"Lord Davenport-Witt?"

"Yes, Lord Davenport-Witt." Mr. Dubois' disdain for Charles was apparent.

"Why do you think he's guilty?" Ginger asked carefully.

Mr. Dubois subconsciously ran a finger along the scar on his face. "For one, Beaulieu was killed at his wedding reception."

"Circumstantial."

"Both he and Beaulieu had been involved with Miss Vasseur."

"I thought you and Miss Vasseur had been involved."

"That is a lie. It was Beaulieu!"

Ginger picked up the plate of sandwich triangles and held it for Mr. Dubois. "Would you care for a sandwich, Mr. Dubois?" She hoped to diffuse her guest's anger. And she needed a moment to contemplate why he would lie. Mr. Dubois had been in love with Miss Vasseur. Ginger had a clear memory of Mr. Dubois asking for her during her triage visit.

Mr. Dubois hesitated, then plucked two sandwich triangles off the plate. After a bite, he said, "Now, the new Lady Davenport-Witt is lovely. Such a shame she married a cad."

"Please forgive my confusion," Ginger said, "but the earl invited you to his wedding, and you accepted the invitation. Why would you do such a thing if you hold him in such low esteem?"

"Webster wanted to go, and I had not seen Beaulieu in a while. I came for them."

"Would you excuse me for a moment, Mr. Dubois?" She patted her stomach. "Lately, nature calls more often."

"Certainly," he said.

Ginger had left the plate of sandwiches in reach, and Mr. Dubois helped himself to more.

Ginger's heels clip-clopped loudly on the marble floor in the corridor. She returned through the dining room, a shorter route to the sitting room, keeping to the tips of her toes, her steps quieter on the wooden floors. She paused outside the swinging door between the dining room and sitting room and took a breath. She wasn't sure what she'd expected to learn by inviting Mr. Dubois for tea, and now she found she regretted the gesture. She'd have to come up with a polite way to suggest he leave.

Carefully pushing the door open a crack—Ginger was thankful Pippins kept the swinging door well oiled—she peeked in. Her experience proved that people behaved differently when they didn't know they were being observed, and Mr. Dubois didn't fail her. After checking to confirm that he was alone in the room, he—to Ginger's great shock—got to his feet and took several steps to view the nearly nude form in the *The Mermaid*, a Waterhouse painting that hung over the mantel.

As Ginger had suspected, Pierre Dubois could walk!

Just as Ginger let the door slip closed, she heard Felicia's voice.

"Oh, I thought Mrs. Reed would be here."

Mr. Dubois answered smoothly, "She 'as taken a trip to zee ladies. Wait wiz me, my lady."

Ginger's heart jumped to her throat. Pierre Dubois was dangerous, and now Felicia was within his grasp.

Ginger hurried to her study and retrieved her Remington derringer from the desk drawer. Garters came in handy, not just for holding up one's stockings but also for concealing a weapon. Ginger secured the palm-sized pistol—a gift from her late husband—in her garter. Pippins—who seemed to have a sixth sense—appeared in the doorway. "Is everything to your satisfaction, madam."

Her eyes darted to the telephone on her desk. "Please ring Scotland Yard. Tell them it's an emergency!"

Ginger returned to the corridor, purposely stepping loudly along the marble flooring. She plastered on a smile and entered the sitting room.

"Oh, there you are," Felicia said. "Grandmama left to visit Mrs. Schofield. Charles won't be picking me up for another hour. You and Mr. Dubois must keep me from dying of boredom."

Ginger intended to keep Felicia from dying by any means.

"Do you like to read, Mr. Dubois?" Felicia asked.

"Occasionally."

"I find it such a marvellous way to pass the time. I'm reading Mrs. Christie's *The Murder on the Links*. I find I want to, in turns, visit Paris and take up golf." After a chuckle she added, "I'm a mystery writer myself, though—"

Ginger cleared her throat, signalling with her look that the appropriateness of the subject was in question.

Felicia shifted in her seat. "Oh, yes, but that's boring. I read something interesting in the morning paper. Can you believe that someone in Montreal punched the magician Harry Houdini in the stomach? And I thought Canadians were quiet and reserved."

Ginger needed to seat Felicia further from Mr. Dubois.

"Felicia, darling, would you mind pouring us some drinks?" The stocked sideboard sat against the wall on the opposite side of the room. She smiled at Mr. Dubois. "Certainly, it's not too early for a cocktail?"

"When one spends time with Harry Webster, one believes zat no time ees too early."

Ginger laughed at Mr. Dubois' attempt at humour. "What would you like? Felicia is a star at preparing cocktails."

"Very well, a martini would suit me fine."

"I'll have soda water," Ginger said lightly. "Perhaps you could turn on the wireless as well?"

"I'm not sure what you have servants for," Felicia said, "but, all right."

Ginger returned to the settee. "How long will you stay in London, Mr. Dubois?"

"Not much longer. I 'ave almost accomplished everysing I've wanted to do."

Revenge killings of Jean-Claude Beaulieu and

Estelle Vasseur? How clever to make everyone believe he was held captive in a wheelchair. He could've lured Mr. Beaulieu to the terrace, stepped out of his chair, and entered a wrestling match that ended with a gun going off. Then, before anyone arrived on the scene to investigate, he was safely in his chair at the step. Ginger had wondered why he'd looked rather dishevelled and had chalked it up to the effects of an evening of drinking.

What concerned her now? Mr. Dubois' suggestion he wasn't quite finished. Was Charles the next target?

Mr. Dubois' eyes were glued to Felicia as he watched her deliver the drinks, first to Ginger, then to himself.

"*Merci*, my lady," he said. "I 'ope you do not mind me saying zat I am surprised Davenport-Witt 'as let you out of his sight—such a beautiful woman— and so quickly after your wedding."

Felicia blushed. She was about to take the chair next to Mr. Dubois when Ginger made a show of spilling her drink. "Oh no! Felicia, please find a cloth in the sideboard. We must clean this before it stains."

"Shouldn't I ring for Lizzie or one of the new maids?"

"It'll take too long. Please, there's a cloth in the drawer."

With a huff, Felicia acquiesced. "Very well."

The ruse had got Felicia out of harm's way. If only she could get her out of the room. Ginger didn't dare leave Mr. Dubois alone, as he might take the opportunity to leave his chair.

As it was, he seemed to be growing restless. The police were on their way, and Ginger only had to hold his attention for a short while longer.

Felicia found the cloth and sat beside Ginger, dabbing at the wet spots on the settee. She chastised. "This pregnancy is really making you clumsy."

When Felicia finished mopping up the spilled drink, Mr. Dubois held up his empty glass. "Eef I could bother you for a second round, Lady Davenport-Witt? Mrs. Reed ees correct; you are very good at making drinks."

"Certainly."

Felicia stepped towards Mr. Dubois. Just as her hand touched his glass, the police motorcars sped to a stop at the kerb, and naturally, she stopped to stare out the window. Mr. Dubois did the same.

With the swiftness of a cobra, Mr. Dubois sprang to his feet, gripped Felicia by the wrist, and pulled her back to his chest.

The empty glass clanged onto the floor.

Felicia yelled out in surprise. "Mr. Dubois!"

In a swift motion, while Mr. Dubois' eyes were trained on Felicia, Ginger reached under her skirts and palmed the Remington.

"Shut up!" Mr. Dubois held Felicia tightly, then produced a flick knife—perhaps the same one that had taken Miss Vasseur's life—and held it to Felicia's neck. Over Felicia's head, he glared at Ginger, who'd jumped to her feet.

"Stay back, or I swear, I'll slit 'er sroat."

Felicia's eyes were wide with fear, but to her credit, she kept her composure. It wasn't the first time since working with Ginger that her life had been in peril. Thankfully, the scarf Felicia wore around her neck provided a buffer from the flick knife's edge, an advantage of which Mr. Dubois seemed unaware.

Ginger locked eyes with her and spoke reassuringly. "It's going to be all right."

"Ha!" Mr. Dubois said. "Call off zee 'ounds , Mrs. Reed. Tell zem you are mistaken. Or zat I am gone. Do it, or she dies!"

Bracing herself with a wide-legged stance, Ginger aimed her pistol, holding it in front of her with both hands, her arms straight.

"You might not know this about me, Mr. Dubois," she said, cocking the gun. "But I'm an excellent shot. This bullet will embed itself in your forehead at the slightest twitch. Tell me you'll let Lady Davenport-Witt go, and your life will be spared."

For now.

*P*ierre Dubois merely laughed. "I suppose we shall see who blinks first, no?"

Ginger held Felicia's gaze, willing her to remain brave. A change of subject was needed now—a diversion.

Ginger reverted to French. "How long have you been able to walk, Mr. Dubois?"

Pierre Dubois replied in French as well. "Two years." He stood as he gripped Felicia, but his legs shook as if he wasn't used to bearing his weight. "It took me years longer of practising in the privacy of my room, enduring *agony* to get to the place where I could take a few steps. Then over time, I could do more and more."

"You can walk as far as from the guest house to the front door of Witt House, I presume."

"And back, Mrs. Reed," he said with a note of pride.

"You blamed Jean-Claude Beaulieu," Ginger said, "didn't you?" Known to Ginger during the war years simply as Claude, she'd heard a rumour that he'd run off on the night of the raid, failing to assist his fellow men.

"He left me to die," Pierre said. "He'd left all of us to die. So nice of him to be the only one to walk away without a scratch. He liked to claim to be a hero, but those of us who were there, the only two left to speak about it, me and Spider, know the truth. Beaulieu wasn't a hero; he was a traitor! He had to have let the Boche know we were coming. It's the only reason the mission would have failed. It was my burning desire for revenge that drove me to push through my pain and walk again so that I could gain my vengeance." He smiled wickedly. "You should've seen Beaulieu's face when I came for him in the garden."

"You dislocated his shoulder."

"Oui. My legs may be weak, but my arms are strong from pushing the wretched chair about." His grip on Felicia grew tighter with his anger. Felicia whimpered, her eyes wide with fear as they appealed to Ginger.

Ginger tried a softer approach. "Mr. Dubois, why not let Lady Davenport-Witt go? We can talk about it over tea."

"Ha. You think me a fool. I am *not*. We will walk out of here, the lady with me, and you will drive me to the aerodrome. Your sister will be safe when I am on board, in the air, and flying back to France."

Ginger now knew that Pierre Dubois was delusional. There was no way he could escape England in this fashion and at such short notice.

"Very well," she said. "But only if you let Lady Davenport-Witt go. I will drive you to the aerodrome myself, no questions asked."

"Why should I believe you?"

"Because I believed you, Pantin. Do you remember when I came to visit you in the hospital in Amiens?"

His expression softened a little. "Oui. You were truly kind, Mademoiselle LaFleur."

From the corner of her eye, Ginger saw Basil through the crack in the door. He stared back with narrowed eyes. Ginger subtly shook her head. If she couldn't talk Pierre down, he would die in her sitting room. Not only would that be a shame for him, but it would also make a terrible mess on the Persian carpet.

"Pierre, we had been friends. We are still friends, no?"

Pierre relaxed his hold, and Ginger thought the worst was behind them, but then she overplayed her hand.

"I helped you by looking for Estelle Vasseur and Spider."

"But you didn't find, Estelle, did you!" he spat. "Not that it matters. I eventually tracked her down. Do you know, she never once came to visit me in triage?"

Ginger felt for the man; how broken-hearted he'd been to find his love had moved on and hadn't even come to see how he was faring. Not even once.

However, it didn't justify murder.

"You sent her a note to meet you at Charles' house, using Mr. Hughes as a ruse."

Mr. Dubois snorted. "She wouldn't come to see me, not with legs that didn't work. But Hughes, he was yet unconquered."

"So, you killed her."

"She betrayed me!" He tightened his hold on Felicia. "With *her* earl!"

The door banged opened, and a furious Charles

Davenport-Witt stood in the entrance. "Dubois! I'll wring your neck with my bare hands!"

His pronouncement startled Mr. Dubois, giving Felicia a chance to step to the side, throwing the weakening man off-balance and loosening his hold. In a flash, Charles tore Felicia out of Mr. Dubois' grasp—Ginger surmised that Charles' hadn't seen the danger of the knife—and knocked his feet out from beneath him for good measure.

Mr. Dubois rubbed his leg as he called out in pain. His eyes darted about like a frightened animal. Basil stepped into the room, but before he could accost him, Mr. Dubois held the knife to his own neck.

"Stay away!"

Besides the *mess,* if Mr. Dubois took his life, there wouldn't be a trial or proper justice for Mr. Beaulieu and Miss Vasseur.

"I devoted my life to the cause," Mr. Dubois said. "And what did it get me? Misery! A life of pity. While Beaulieu strutted about like a proud peacock, a new girl on his arm every month, boasting about war exploits he'd never actually taken part in. He was a liar and a cheat."

"Mr. Dubois," Ginger said softly, "I'm going to

lower my pistol." She slowly placed the gun on the coffee table. "Please, put your knife down."

"Pierre?"

Ginger turned to the voice, surprised to see that Harry Webster had entered the room. "I'd like a drink," he said as if he hadn't come upon a man so distraught, he was prepared to take his own life. "Wouldn't you, Dubois?"

The pain behind Mr. Webster's eyes showed he suddenly realised the gravity of the situation. Ginger's heart bled for the man. If it were Felicia in Mr. Dubois' place, broken and guilty of a heinous crime, she would be shattered. That the man known as Spider could paste on a smile and enter the charade was a testament to his talent as a spy and his loyalty as a friend.

"Come on, chum," he said. Mr. Webster helped Mr. Dubois into the wheelchair like Ginger had seen him do many times. "For old time's sake."

Mr. Dubois' dark eyes grew glassy as he considered his one loyal friend. Mr. Webster's eyes glistened as well.

"*Oui, mon ami*," Mr. Dubois said. Once he'd settled back into the chair he added, "I'd like a bit of whisky."

CHAPTER TWENTY-FOUR

Basil hurried to Ginger's side, and she embraced him. He gripped her with all the emotion of a man who had watched his beloved walk towards a cliff and had stopped her in the nick of time. Grabbing her hands in both of his, Basil ducked to stare into her lovely green eyes.

"Ginger, I know you can't help yourself, but please, please, just stay out of harm's way for once."

Ginger smiled sympathetically. "Oh, Basil, I don't do it on purpose. But in this instance, I wasn't the one in true peril."

A similar reunion was going on with Charles and Felicia. Felicia had regained colour in her face. Charles was promising to sweep her away on their wedding journey as soon as possible.

Webster and Dubois were at the side table where Webster had helped himself to a decanter of whisky and poured two glasses. As if the stand-off hadn't occurred, they drank like mates in a pub.

Braxton and Newman, who'd been waiting with Basil and Charles, stood by the door.

After a few moments, Basil said, "Arrest Mr. Dubois."

"On what grounds?" Braxton asked.

"For the murders of Mr. Beaulieu and Miss Vasseur."

Dubois offered his wrists without resistance, and Braxton clipped on the handcuffs. As Newman pushed the wheelchair out of the room, Dubois looked over his shoulder at Webster. "Farewell, *mon ami.*"

When he had gone, Webster crumpled into a chair and pressed his palms against his eyes.

Ginger approached, putting a hand on his shoulder. "I'm so sorry, Mr. Webster. You were an excellent friend to Mr. Dubois."

"Thank you, Mrs. Reed. Sadly, it appears that my friendship wasn't good enough."

"The war has damaged us all," Ginger said. "Some more than others."

"I'll see myself out," Mr. Webster said.

Ginger took his hand. "Shall we ring for a taxicab?"

"Thank you, madam, but I think a good walk will do me good."

"Do take care, Mr. Webster," she said.

He nodded, then left.

"I can't help but feel sorry for the bloke," Basil said. "Forging a good friendship in this life is rare."

Ginger agreed. Losing a good friend in this way was doubly tragic.

Charles poured them a round of drinks, Ginger taking soda water only, as was her habit with the baby on the way.

"What's going to happen to him now?" Felicia asked after a drink.

"Inquest, trial, conviction," Charles said soberly. "Hanging."

"You say that as if you've never cared for the man," Felicia said with surprising insight. "Why did you invite him to our wedding?"

"Out of a sense of duty, I suppose," Charles sighed. "I wasn't there when Dubois was captured, and I always felt a bit guilty about having escaped injury during the war. I regret inviting him now, of course. For all involved. And I'm sorry for the man."

"It was such good luck that Mr. Webster suddenly dropped in," Felicia said.

Basil patted Charles on the back. "It was hardly luck. Our old chap here instructed Pippins to ring him up."

Felicia stared at her new husband with growing admiration. "Charles! How very perceptive of you."

"I simply counted on the friendship I knew the two of them shared."

"One question remains," Ginger said, catching Charles' eye. "How did Pierre Dubois come to have your service pistol?"

Charles' countenance darkened. "I've racked my brain for an answer to that question as well," he said. "And the only thing I can think of is that he stole it from me."

Ginger restrained herself from displaying disbelief. "And how would that have transpired?"

Charles took a long swig of his drink before answering. "After the war, I visited Dubois at a rehabilitation centre." He cast a glance at Felicia. "This part of the story is unsavoury."

Felicia patted his arm. "Don't hold back on my account, love."

"Very well," Charles continued. "Dubois begged

me to relieve him of his misery; he could not face a life in a wheelchair."

Ginger's heart skipped a beat. "He wanted you to—"

"Yes. Of course, I refused. The request so shook me,I grabbed my jacket that hung on a rack by the door and left. I clearly remember tossing it into the back of my motorcar, and with the weather growing warmer, leaving it there for a few months."

"Are you saying someone took your pistol at the rehabilitation centre?" Basil said, "And you didn't notice it?"

Charles ran a hand through his hair as he let out a hard breath. "I know it's difficult to believe, but those first years after the war were intense. With all the clearing up and tearing down of old barracks and makeshift hospitals, I honestly forgot about it."

"What about when it was time to surrender it to the government?" Ginger asked.

"I had to admit to them I'd lost track of it," Charles said sheepishly. "It wasn't all that uncommon, you know."

He turned to Felicia. "I swear, if I'd known about my pistol's whereabouts or who had it last, I would've said."

Felicia cupped her husband's cheek. "Of course, you would've, love."

Ginger wanted to believe him. However, if Charles had felt indebted to Mr. Dubois in any way, he might've been tempted to turn a blind eye and leave his pistol behind on purpose.

Felicia faced Ginger and Basil. "Mr. Dubois must've stolen Charles' pistol, or perhaps a sympathetic nurse helped him out by taking it."

Ginger found it difficult to accept this story. A spy didn't just misplace a pistol, but she couldn't express that belief aloud. Besides, she refused to judge anyone for what they might have done in the throes of a terrible and traumatizing war and its aftermath. She was grateful that Mr. Dubois hadn't made Charles an accessory to his death, and ultimately, she had to place some trust in Felicia's new husband, for Felicia's sake. No one was perfect, after all. Perhaps during the turmoil at the war's end, Charles really had lost sight of his pistol. Ginger hoped so.

Regardless, she had to accept that, despite being aware of Charles' connection to the British secret service, there was much she'd never fully learn about the man. Such was the nature of the institution.

Charles took Felicia by the hand. "Let us go,

love, and forget about all this horror. Greece awaits us."

Basil and Ginger said goodbye to Felicia and Charles, sending them off with wishes of safe travels and good health, and suddenly the two of them were alone in the room.

"Basil?"

"Yes, love?"

Ginger smiled. He was looking at her again with eyes of fondness and adoration. "You were off somewhere."

"No, no, I assure you, I'm all here," Basil returned quickly, smiling in return. "You were saying . . ."

"Another case solved."

She stepped into Basil as he pulled her back into his arms. "You were stupendous, once again," he said. Then with a grin, he whispered, "*Mademoiselle.*"

Ginger stilled, but he rubbed her back in reassurance. Ginger knew that Basil had accepted for some time that she had had an involvement in the war in an official capacity that kept her from telling him everything he wanted to know about her. Over time, some layers of her mysterious past had been revealed —not of her doing.

He'd never know everything, a fact Ginger knew drove him crazy, but he loved her and often commended her for her courage, both then and now. And she hoped that knowing that she'd had special training, something that had saved both their lives, occasionally brought him comfort.

However, her past and his knowledge of it were the least of her concerns at the moment. Ginger pressed her palms to her protruding belly and gasped. The alarm in her eyes made Basil's heart stop.

"What is it, love?" He reached for her arm. "Are you all right?"

Ginger shook her head. "Basil," she murmured. "It's too soon."

If you enjoyed reading *Murder in Belgravia* please help others enjoy it too.

Recommend it: Help others find the book by recommending it to friends, readers' groups, discussion boards and by **suggesting it to your local library.**

Review it: Please tell other readers why you liked this book by reviewing it on Amazon or Goodreads.

* No spoilers please *

Don't miss the next Ginger Gold mystery~
MURDER ON MALLOWAN COURT

Murder's afoot!

As Mrs. Ginger Reed~also known as Lady Gold~waits impatiently for the coming of her baby, new neighbours move onto Mallowan Court. The Foote family is very much like Ginger's own, if not the mirror opposite: Mr. and Mrs. Foote an unhappy couple; Mr. Rothwell an aging, irate patriarch; Miss Charlotte, whom Scout finds to be a tantalizing, if confusing specimen of young ladyhood; along with a similar collection of staff.

The sudden passing of a Foote family member is determined to be unsuspicious, but something about this strange family doesn't sit right with Ginger.

When the doctor banishes Ginger to her bed to await the coming birth, she has to depend on the information brought to her by her own faithful staff and family members to prove the crime. But can she keep her own household safe?

Buy on AMAZON or read Free with Kindle Unlimited!

Have you discovered Rosa Reed?
Check out this new, fun 1950s cozy mystery series!

MURDER AT HIGH TIDE
a Rosa Reed Mystery #1

Murder's all wet!

It's 1956 and WPC (Woman Police Constable) Rosa Reed has left her groom at the altar in London. Time spent with her American cousins in Santa Bonita,

California is exactly what she needs to get back on her feet, though the last thing she expected was to get entangled in another murder case!

If you love early rock & roll, poodle skirts, clever who-dun-its, a charming cat and an even more charming detective, you're going to love this new series!

Buy on AMAZON or read Free with Kindle Unlimited!

Sign up for Lee's readers list and gain access to **Ginger Gold's private Journal.** Find out about Ginger's Life before the SS *Rosa* and how she became the woman she has. This is a fluid document that will cover her romance with her late husband Daniel, her time serving in the British secret service during World War One, and beyond. Includes a recipe for Dark Dutch Chocolate Cake!

It begins: **July 31, 1912**

How fabulous that I found this Journal today, hidden in the bottom of my wardrobe. Good old Pippins, our English butler in London, gave it to me as a parting gift when Father whisked me away on our American adventure so he could marry Sally. Pips said it was for me to record my new adventures. I'm ashamed I never even penned one word before today. I think I was just too sad.

This old leather-bound journal takes me back to that emotional time. I had shed enough tears to fill the ocean and I remember telling

Father dramatically that I was certain to cause flooding to match God's. At eight years old I was well-trained in my biblical studies, though, in retro-spect, I would say that I had probably bordered on heresy with my little tantrum.

The first week of my "adventure" was spent with a tummy ache and a number of embarrassing sessions that involved a bucket and Father holding back my long hair so I wouldn't soil it with vomit.

I certainly felt that I was being punished for some reason. Hartigan House—though large and sometimes lonely—was my home and Pips was my good friend. He often helped me to pass the time with games of I Spy and Xs and Os.

"Very good, Little Miss," he'd say with a twinkle in his blue eyes when I won, which I did often. I suspect now that our good butler wasn't beyond letting me win even when unmerited.

Father had got it into his silly head that I needed a mother, but I think the truth was he wanted a wife. Sally, a woman half my father's age, turned out to be a sufficient wife in the end, but I could never claim her as a mother.

Well, Pips, I'm sure you'd be happy to know that things turned out all right here in America.

SUBSCRIBE to read more!
http://www.
leestraussbooks.com/gingergoldjournalsignup/

.

ABOUT THE AUTHOR

Lee Strauss is a USA TODAY bestselling author of The Ginger Gold Mysteries series, The Higgins & Hawke Mystery series, The Rosa Reed Mystery series (cozy historical mysteries), A Nursery Rhyme Mystery series (mystery suspense), The Perception series (young adult dystopian), The Light & Love series (sweet romance), The Clockwise Collection (YA time travel romance), and young adult historical fiction with over a million books read. She has titles published in German, Spanish and Korean, and a growing audio library.

When Lee's not writing or reading she likes to cycle, hike, and stare at the ocean. She loves to drink caffè lattes and red wines in exotic places, and eat dark chocolate anywhere.

For more info on books by Lee Strauss and her social media links, visit leestraussbooks.com.

Did you know you can follow your favourite authors on Bookbub? If you subscribe to Bookbub — (and if you don't, why don't you? - They'll send you daily emails alerting you to sales and new releases on just the kind of books you like to read!) — follow me to make sure you don't miss the next Ginger Gold Mystery!

www.leestraussbooks.com

leestraussbooks@gmail.com

Murder by Plum Pudding

Murder on Fleet Street

Murder at Brighton Beach

Murder in Hyde Park

Murder at the Royal Albert Hall

Murder in Belgravia

Murder on Mallowan Court

LADY GOLD INVESTIGATES (Ginger Gold companion short stories)

Volume 1

Volume 2

Volume 3

Volume 4

HIGGINS & HAWKE MYSTERY SERIES (cozy 1930s historical)

The 1930s meets Rizzoli & Isles in this friendship depression era cozy mystery series.

Death at the Tavern

Death on the Tower

Death on Hanover

Death by Dancing

THE ROSA REED MYSTERIES

(1950s cozy historical)

Murder at High Tide

Murder on the Boardwalk

Murder at the Bomb Shelter

Murder on Location

Murder and Rock 'n Roll

Murder at the Races

Murder at the Dude Ranch

Murder in London

A NURSERY RHYME MYSTERY
SERIES(mystery/sci fi)

Marlow finds himself teamed up with intelligent and savvy Sage Farrell, a girl so far out of his league he feels blinded in her presence - literally - damned glasses! Together they work to find the identity of @gingerbreadman. Can they stop the killer before he strikes again?

Gingerbread Man

Life Is but a Dream

Hickory Dickory Dock

Twinkle Little Star

THE PERCEPTION TRILOGY (YA dystopian mystery)

Zoe Vanderveen is a GAP—a genetically altered person. She lives in the security of a walled city on prime water-front property along side other equally beautiful people with extended life spans. Her brother Liam is missing. Noah Brody, a boy on the outside, is the only one who can help ~ but can she trust him?

Perception

Volition

Contrition

LIGHT & LOVE (sweet romance)

Set in the dazzling charm of Europe, follow Katja, Gabriella, Eva, Anna and Belle as they find strength, hope and love.

Sing me a Love Song

Your Love is Sweet

In Light of Us

Lying in Starlight

PLAYING WITH MATCHES (WW2 history/romance)

A sobering but hopeful journey about how one young German boy copes with the war and propaganda. Based on true events.

A Piece of Blue String (companion short story)

THE CLOCKWISE COLLECTION (YA time travel romance)

Casey Donovan has issues: hair, height and uncontrollable trips to the 19th century! And now this ~ she's accidentally taken Nate Mackenzie, the cutest boy in the school, back in time. Awkward.

Clockwise

Clockwiser

Like Clockwork

Counter Clockwise

Clockwork Crazy

Clocked (companion novella)

<u>Standalones</u>

Seaweed

Love, Tink

www.ingramcontent.com/pod-product-compliance
Lightning Source LLC
Chambersburg PA
CBHW050257110726
47898CB00007B/2446